CW01497453

THE TOWER

Thea Lenarduzzi is a writer, broadcaster and editor. Her debut, *Dandelions*, a family memoir and cultural history of migration between Italy and England, won the 2020 Fitzcarraldo Editions Essay Prize and was shortlisted for the Ackerley Prize for 'literary autobiography of outstanding merit'. *The Tower* is her second book.

'A hybrid, shifting, searching work that applies pressure
to the boundaries between forms before it crosses them,
The Tower asks questions about stories, narrative and
history – and our uneasy inheritance of them – that linger
long after the book's final pages. I couldn't get it out of my
mind.'
—— Helen Charman, author of *Mother State*

'Thea Lenarduzzi works against the grain of her own and
readers' expectations in this graceful book, in which stories
are dismantled so that new truths can be found. Beautifully
considered: *The Tower* is both delicate and wise.'
—— Anne Enright, author of *The Wren, The Wren*

'Life, and writing, can expand from a detail: to which
extent must this detail be personal? In this remarkable
and surprising book, Thea Lenarduzzi wanders through
the many paths of fiction-making, in a literary quest to
find out if the girl in the tower is a romanticized symbol,
an exhausted trope, a resourceful broken archive at the
beginning of a powerful story, hers as much as ours. Truly
fascinating and brimming with intellectual energy.'
—— Claudia Durastanti, author of *Strangers I Know*

'In *The Tower*, Thea Lenarduzzi offers a brilliant and
exacting meditation on the stories we tell about a life – and
the cultural and familial forces of thought that can obscure
self-understanding. Tracing the fate of a young woman
exiled to a stone tower after a tuberculosis diagnosis,
Lenarduzzi braids archival enquiry with imaginative
force, illuminating how the past shapes our present griefs
and inheritances. This is a rare kind of book: intimate yet
capacious, unsettling yet precise in its enquiry into harm,
inheritance and the limits of language. The result is a
profound reckoning with memory and silence: what we
remember, what we omit and why.'
—— Meghan O'Rourke, author of *The Invisible Kingdom*

'*The Tower* is about the allure (and refusal) of certain narratives, about the sublime quest an author takes when she embarks on the act of storytelling. Its form – a composite of fiction, memoir, history – mirrors its subject matter and, excitingly, "stages" its very questions. In this elegantly composed, layered and expansive book, Thea Lenarduzzi articulates something of the mysterious nature of stories while also making an argument for all that is unknowable.'
—— Lauren Aimee Curtis, author of *Strangers at the Port*

'With her sensitive, fable-like unravelling of a mysterious anecdote, Thea Lenarduzzi enlists and subverts all the elements of a gripping story – a secret, a journey, doubt and denouement – to emerge with an intricately crafted meditation on the nature of narrative itself. *The Tower* masterfully loops back on itself and retraces its own steps to uncover the secrets, wishes and fears that lurk in the stories we tell about ourselves, and what draws us to those of others.'
—— Daisy Lafarge, author of *Lovebug*

'A fascinating and shapeshifting book that is simultaneously a literary pursuit and a forensic examination of power, abuse and the human scope for mythologizing. The result is pure magic.'
—— Catherine Taylor, author of *The Stirrings*

'In her second remarkable and equally wise book, Lenarduzzi explores how we shape and share our stories – of ourselves and of others. Some are rooted in truth, others are constructed over generations of telling, and then there are those that relate to the depths of consciousness. She leads us with lyrical and meticulous prose via convincing digressions to an unexpected place to which I feel privileged to have journeyed.'
—— Julia Bueno, author of *Everyone's A Critic*

Praise for *Dandelions*

'*Dandelions* is a book of hauntings, intensely experienced, pierced by occasional terrors, yet irradiated throughout by passionate attachment. Thea Lenarduzzi has spread out before us a feast of sensuous and sensitive, nuanced and deeply appealing testimony to migration, survival and complicated identities at a time when such thoughtfulness is rare and desperately needed.'
— Marina Warner, author of *Sanctuary*

'Beautifully observed and written with heart and an infectious curiosity, Thea Lenarduzzi's *Dandelions* parses the complex ways in which we live out our histories and carry the past within us, through ritual, food, language and legend. Like rifling through an overflowing drawer or opening an ancient photo album, Lenarduzzi unearths glinting gems of family fiction, introducing us to a shifting cast of memorable characters whose journeys, stories and passions it's our joy to share.'
— Francesca Wade, author of *Gertrude Stein: An Afterlife*

'In this subtle and elegant family memoir, Thea Lenarduzzi gathers the ghost seeds between her present life in England and her family's past in Italy. A meditation on roots, inheritance and homesickness, *Dandelions* is also a reminder that what will survive of us is love.'
— Frances Wilson, author of *Electric Spark*

'*Dandelions* is spellbinding. Like the polished beads of a secular rosary, each bearing a remembrance, Lenarduzzi's ancestral memoir conjures intimate histories of migration, love and loss across decades of passages between Italy and England. Her redoubtable grandmother Dirce will lure you in, as she unfolds fragmentary myths with a sly wit, whispering *ascolta*, "listen" – and you won't resist.'
— Anna Della Subin, author of *Accidental Gods*

Fitzcarraldo Editions

THE TOWER

THEA LENARDUZZI

CONTENTS

'I believe this: fairy tales are true.'
— Italo Calvino (1956)

'But why bring it all up now, after so many years?
She must have a book out.'
— Anon (2024)

Once I read a story about a woman who became trapped in a suffocating vision of the afterlife, condemned to wander through time and relive her memories on a loop for ever more, so that after a while she was merely an exhausted observer of her own life and fate.

'You think the past affects the future,' a character says to her as she confronts for the hundredth time a particularly painful episode. 'Has it never struck you that the future may affect the past?'

I had never thought of time as so plainly a two-way trip, and of cause and effect as return passengers. Though I couldn't work out if it was for good or ill, I didn't doubt for a minute that the assessment was completely and complicatedly true. Were it not, I would probably be telling you a different story now.

But before I came to know this story properly, before I came to, I *think*, understand it, the one I'm about to tell you, about a girl – or a woman – and a tower on a hill, I didn't hear how, in it, the past and the future spoke to each other. I didn't see that the past was only what it was, a tragedy, because the future had conspired to make it so. I didn't see how, because of this whispered communion between the past and the future (a future which was, in any case, already the past to some other future), two lives became joined together, easily, as if instinctively, as if they always had been, eliding great differences, to speak as one.

Or howl. A howl of all time, like a discordant chorus cast from the heights of Babel across a flooded land, where the ground mirrors the sky and no one can be sure which way is up or down, which way back and which forwards, what happened and what was only in the mind.

I fear I haven't explained it at all clearly. But I hope you'll come to see what I mean. Perhaps for now I should simply say that we don't always tell the story we want to tell. We can't always choose our place in it, nor how it ends, or if it even does. That, reader, is the stuff of fiction.

I.

A GIRL

Years and years ago, a man told a woman a story about a girl who died in a tower, in a place hundreds of miles north from them and more than a century past. From that moment, every few months, the woman would lead the man through the hoops of the story. *But so she died in there...? Did someone tell you this or was there a plaque, something written...?* They must have had the same conversation a hundred times or more, his words becoming fewer and flightier with each retelling, the weighted silence of brain-racking and hesitation taking over.

It was so long ago, he'd say, even in the early days when it wasn't.

Information was nibbled away by the moths of forgetfulness, doubt and distraction, and she did nothing to stop holes forming. She – let's call her T – wrote no details down, which went against her usual habit of capturing a good story, with a half-thought that she'd make use of it in some shape, at some point (you should know she made a living telling other people's stories). The more stubborn elements – I'm not sure I can say facts – belonged to a different register, like a few scattered stones that might be bits of bone or a trick of the light that could be a human face suspended in air.

In the beginning this is what she knew: one autumn, her boyfriend, as he was at the time, went on a trip with his father, walking in the north of the country, where they encountered a strange structure, a little tower; 'a folly', he called it. Back home, he showed her a photograph of it on his phone and, even then, she remembered wishing he hadn't. An octagonal tower on two levels: mostly glass upstairs and too-white masonry below, beneath a steep slate roof. The tower's banal appearance didn't seem to match his story, she thought, about a young woman with tuberculosis who was confined for three years by her father, and died there sometime in the early 1900s.

I called it his story just now, but she had claimed it as her own before he had stopped talking, before even she was aware of having done so.

Over the years, she found online more images like the one he had shown her, snapped by ramblers and posted with sparse and sceptical commentary. *It is commonly thought... Locals believe... They say...* As if those people weren't themselves saying it, some part of them believing it, or wanting to. She wondered why they distanced themselves like that, as if they were looking down from a great height. She read them all, must have found every blog there was to be found, gulped them like cheap lemonade on a hot day. They gave her a rush. In one image, apparently photocopied and then scanned from a newspaper of the 1940s and so grainy it was almost pointillist, a cow called Daisy had found her way into the tower and peered out of an upstairs window, as if deciding what to wear for the weather. In another, the tower was in ruins, only half of the base still standing, its stone unmasked and its doorway gaping. Like an open mouth, she said to herself. Like an open grave.

For some time after the events of our story had run their course, she wished the tower still looked that way, undistinguished and grey, fuzzed by moss. She wished they had never rebuilt it, reconstructing the past, Disneyfying tragedy for just anyone walking by to notice; an ambush on the feelings and imagination, a trap for the vulnerable or foolish. She spent nights willing the thing to crumble again, picturing stones in the grass without apparent pattern or purpose. If the tower disappeared, she thought, perhaps everything else would, too.

The first time she found the girl she was 'Anne', a name identical in sound to the indefinite article. *An*, not *the*: unknown, one of many, undifferentiated and so easy to forget.

The next time, she found 'Ann', then 'Annie', 'Elizabeth Anne', 'Elizabeth Annie', and almost every combination of those names, the most common of the day. Annie stuck, perhaps because it was more familiar, perhaps because it made her sound little and in need of care. One day she found a birth date of 1890; another, of 1889.

At some point she found her in 1911, age twenty-one and single, living in a big house with her father Charles Edward (age fifty-seven), mother Alice (fifty-six), older siblings Charles Edgar (twenty-five) and Emmeline Alice (twenty-three), the cook Margaret, and three servants: Ella, Bessie and Laura. Twenty rooms were counted on the premises, not including the scullery, landings, lobbies, closets and bathrooms, so T knew she was in the presence of significant wealth. The father's occupation was given as 'Farmer, sheep and dairy', which made sense in that rural part of the world, up there where the grasses of the moors fed the ewes, whose wool fed the mills, whose profits and wages fed whole villages and towns; but it threw her because she had read elsewhere, she couldn't recall where precisely, that he was a medical man, a pharmacist. Which suggested quite a different world.

Months, maybe a year later, alone in her apartment on a rainy winter's night, she spiralled deeper into time and found Annie in 1901, age eleven, in that same house. There, her father's status was confirmed, and it lifted her as if she had spotted a lost key glinting between floorboards: 'Retired chemist', from the capital city of the neighbouring county no less, not long arrived in those parts. She wondered what the locals had made of these outsiders, of this man from the city who could retire young to play at farming. She imagined that's what they said as they looked at his clothes, his hands, and oh just the air around him, smiling to themselves.

Annie's brother wasn't listed among the residents of the manor in 1901, so she assumed he was away at boarding school. He would have been fifteen. Two other siblings were present, though: Frances (nineteen) and Kathleen (five). By the 1911 record Frances must have been away running her own home, while Kathleen, she decided, would probably have been sent to some kind of finishing school around the time she turned fourteen. She knew they hadn't died in the intervening years because in the census – that's where she found the records, I should have said – beside their mother's name and the number of years of marriage (thirty), she found the story of a life distilled and tabulated: Total Children Born Alive (5), Children Still Living (5), Children Who Have Died (0). That's almost all T ever came to know about the mother, Alice.

All these thoughts – contextual, peripheral – seemed to fall into place quite readily, in the way that it's always easiest to put together the outer edges of a jigsaw puzzle. You do it almost without looking at the pieces, your attention already focused on the missing heart of the picture.

What you have to understand is that, until now, none of T's research, to use a term too grand, took much time. There was nothing sustained or methodical about it; it was almost unconscious, a kind of tic. We're talking about minutes, sometimes seconds, snatched here and there over the course of several years, generally on her phone, between meetings, on a train, in a bar waiting for a friend.

Tabs left open in the background, often for weeks on end, a carousel of wonderings half indulged. Searches were frequently curtailed by subscriptions and memberships she didn't have and didn't want to pay for because she wasn't yet sure if it was worth it. By which she meant: if Annie was worth it.

But something curious was happening. In long periods during which T seemed to forget Annie entirely, she was accruing within her, silently depositing particles, details here and there falling into place, so that each time T looked for her again, prompted by who knows what, a book she had read, a change in the weather, she was more present than before; less past, as it were. The recall was that much quicker. It was far-fetched, T would have said so herself, but she started to think that maybe Annie was buried in the stuff of her own life somehow, like the DNA of a distant aunt, and that with each thrust of the shovel she was getting nearer, that eventually she would feel the scrape of relativity. And it made no sense – she knew it – because how can a person feel close to someone they have never known?

She began to picture Annie, to see her everywhere, although she was rarely the same person twice. One melancholy Saturday, in an art gallery shop in a coastal town, she was Gwen John's dark-haired convalescent, identity otherwise unknown, in a shapeless navy smock, her eyes cast down to a book in her lap so that you couldn't tell if she was awake or asleep. Sometime later, she came to her again, a vision as she walked the dog along the edge of a rain-swollen river: a late flowering pre-Raphaelite, a wan and watery Ophelia, with auburn hair swept back and gathered at her crown in a style she had once seen referred to as 'Reverie'.

She tried to paint her one day, in weak washes of

watercolour, to see who or what would come out. It was the first thing she had painted in a decade or more; she could never find the time. Annie's face came out as a pale pink bloom, with two dark smears for eyes and a mouth like a bruise. She set her to dry by the window, then pressed her crinkled skin for a week under a tower of the heaviest books she could find.

III.

At some point she found herself looking at a picture – a postcard, actually – in which the family's manor, set on a low hill, was surrounded on three sides by large oaks and beeches, their foliage skimming the ground like heavy flounced skirts. All was black and white, but the silvery brightness of a cloudless sky reflected in the roof slates and the bleached, patchy lawn in the foreground suggested sunshine, heat. The house was two-tone stone, pale edges framing dark walls, with huge windows looking onto a sweet, romantic garden full of elegantly sculpted shrubs, and beyond, across the estate, to the spot where she, the observer, was notionally standing. A watermark named the photography studio of Francis Frith, an entrepreneur who set out to capture on film every town and village in the land, capitalizing on new technology that made each image cheaply and infinitely reproducible. He shrank the world and sold it back piecemeal to the people who owned it.

Online, in a regional newspaper, she found an article describing how, in 1893, a local chemist had bought the old house, together with its land and more from the neighbours. Ten years later, he erected a large mansion incorporating the original house and commissioned extensive gardens, an orangery and a sweeping drive fringed with tall, graceful trees. It seemed astonishing to T that a pharmacist could afford such excess. 'The lifestyle of the family was very grand,' she read. 'It was said that his daughters always wore fur coats.' This was not the first time she had heard of the women's furs, and each time she caught the half-whisper of the town gossip, a mixture of admiration and judgement undimmed by a century's passing. A raised eyebrow, a curled lip.

Almost before she knew what she was doing she had composed an email to a group of historians based up there, informing them that she was an author writing a book about the family (she didn't specify Annie, I can't say why) and would appreciate whatever assistance they could provide. At that point it felt like playing a harmless game, just a little lie to take her to the next level. Had she stopped to reflect, she would have already felt the first signs of fiction hardening into fact. There was an inevitability about it. She hit send.

About a month later – you'll see that nothing happened very quickly, at first – the local historians sent her maps and articles, including a notice placed in a local newspaper in 1905 on behalf of Charles, in which contractors were invited to tender for extensive work on the site, involving the demolition of old buildings and rebuilding with 'EXTENSIVE ADDITIONS, NEW WING and TOWER'. There was also mention of a new tennis lawn, gate pillars and wrought iron gates, and a stone 'Look-out Tower' to be built on the hill beyond the trees. It seemed fair to expect such works to have taken three or so years to finish, so the date seemed to tally with information T had found elsewhere suggesting that Annie entered the tower at the age of eighteen. Allowing for her unsettled date of birth, that would have been around 1908. She pondered a map showing the raised mound on which the tower came to sit, fringed by dense woodland that (an adjoining article said) gave the estate its name, a compound of the Old Norse words for 'oak' and 'hillside'. Somewhere nearby, she gathered, was an oak tree dating to the first half of the fourteenth century. She traced the river with her finger as it curved around the land and fell off the edge of the page like a waterfall.

She wondered at what point in the construction of the

tower it had become apparent to Charles that it might be repurposed. Maybe he knew it all along; perhaps Annie was already ill in 1905 when the works began, perhaps she had suffered as a child. But he could never have publicly declared the tower's true destiny as a kind of private sanatorium, and that the only person looking out of those high wrap-around windows would be Annie. A map drawn up in 1909 didn't show the tower at all although she knew it would have been there by then, and the secrecy made sense: the more people knew about it, the more they would have meddled and flocked to see for themselves this real-life Lady of Shalott.

From those maps and plans of bricks and trees, however, she could glean no trace of human character beyond the ostentation of Charles. Every fixture, every finial, was him. Of Annie there was nothing.

How, she wondered, do you tell the story of someone who simply isn't there, of whom there is no evidence of body or spirit beyond a pocketful of unsure words carried by forgetful walkers, half lost to the northern winds?

Perhaps you don't, said a voice, a warning. But it was so meek, so quiet; so easy not to hear amid the clamour of the other voices, all of which told her to dig deeper, cast her net wider, seek sustenance from the lives of others. To beg, borrow, steal.

.

One night she put her daughter, A, to bed, heated some soup and settled down to read. Her husband was out and the dog they called 'the wolf', for appearance more than temperament, had taken himself to the front door, where he would keep watch until everyone was where they were supposed to be. To the sound of A's rhythmic breathing and the monitor's static, she opened tab after tab on her laptop, about the most popular magazines of Annie's day, common hobbies for Edwardian young women, the social prospects for those with wealth and taste; about piano exercises, embroidery, scrapbooks and watercolour painting, and how a 'good' girl of the early 1900s should aim to walk up to two hours each day. She read that Victorian mothers like Alice were responsible for their daughters' first lessons in femininity, for instilling ideals of self-sacrifice and subservience to father, husband, brother and nation, before the child knew the difference between night and day. T knew it started long before all that, in the womb.

Women's interests and abilities were of secondary concern, she read, if they were of any concern at all. Only a few 'exceptional' women of the time rebelled against expectations, the historians said. A handful of anomalies pitted against the weight of scientific and medical research that purported to show, through various measurements of skull capacity or brain-body ratio or some other make-believe, that the female sex was inherently weaker in almost every way.

'Without a doubt there exist some distinguished women, very superior to the average man,' a famous physician once said, 'but they are as exceptional as the birth of any monstrosity, as, for example, of a gorilla with two heads; consequently, we may neglect them entirely.' The majority took inferiority into their bones, Annie most likely among them.

It didn't surprise T, of course, that control was a prominent feature in the lives of young women at the turn of the twentieth century; any hierarchy, whether of sex or race or class, relied on careful surveillance, and she had seen and read enough, lived years enough in her own body, to understand how that surveillance was internalized by the subject herself. The previous night she had watched a clunky television drama about a distant island and an institution for 'fallen women', a mother-and-baby home, in which the protagonist, a 'penitent', was told by a nun, 'This isn't a prison, you can leave anytime you want'; but she never did. It couldn't be true, T thought, that detail – there were locked doors and windows in those places, and cruelty calculated precisely to prevent flight – but she saw why the scriptwriters wrote it into the story. Some truths were sensed not proven.

No, what surprised her was how readily even the most benign pleasure became an opportunity to observe and critique. Pastimes such as needlework, T read, were encouraged by parents 'only in part for their pedagogical value; they were used as well to instil cleanliness, caution, and concentration'. The fear of grubby smudges on white lace; of a pricked finger; of a freely wandering mind. Parents would 'open children's letters, superintend their reading, chaperone their visitors, inspect their underwear'.

It went without saying that Annie kept a diary. According to one historian, diaries mining the inner self 'became almost obligatory companions to a class endowed with a modicum of leisure'. They were intended as an exercise in how to be good, a demonstration of sustained virtue, renewed daily. In an article in a scholarly journal, T read that a new diary was a common gift from parent to child on a birthday or at Christmas, so that lively thoughts and observations, about the weather, say, or a trip to the coast, might be disciplined. A diligently kept diary could, so they thought, help to snuff out selfishness and rebelliousness by providing a space in which such undesirable impulses might be contained and worked through until morality prevailed. This was especially important for girls, who could not be trusted to overcome without guidance their baser urges. In fact, it was not really at all for boys, in whom the same urges were given free reign, an entire empire made theirs to gallop across beneath a never-setting sun.

But a diary could also mean the unravelling of all that. It could be an escape to a higher plane of self-substantiation, where ideas and impressions were allowed to breathe, evolve, spread. Some parents and educators worried that the diary could then become a surrogate for fabulous tales, a breeding ground for inappropriate feelings, that feminine observation turned in on itself would necessarily degenerate into self-absorption. What they feared most was that, writing alone in her room, a girl might feel able to express her thoughts about life and those around her; that she might, in putting pen to paper, bring another version of herself into being, a character – a heroine perhaps – beyond reach of parental sanction, in search of a story to call her own. 'Almost all diaries contain at least one moment of a confessional nature,' T read in one or other of the historical accounts, 'sometimes crossed out, sometimes written down the spine in minute handwriting, sometimes just left dangerously on the page.' She remembered a line from Virginia Woolf, a dedicated diarist herself, who said that, 'Nothing has happened until it has been described.' And once described, there was no going back.

Several hours had passed in the kitchen. Half a bowl of soup had gone cold, and T's head was a surreal mixture of educational theory and crochet. She was not sure she had used her time well, if she was any closer to Annie than before. She turned out the lights and crept upstairs, pausing for a moment at A's door to listen to her gentle wheezes unfiltered, a sound like shallow waves over shingle. As she brushed her teeth and stared at her reflection in the bathroom cabinet, lit by a weak nightlight, she found Annie. She saw her sitting in her bedroom at a small rosewood desk set in the recess of a window that looked across the thirsty lawns. Her head was bowed and at a slight angle, one ear tilted down towards the page as if listening for each word before it rose to the nib of her pen like sap, liquid potential. Her hair was up, revealing the fine tendons of her neck, and that felt like an important detail, somehow.

She could have been writing anything: a picture-postcard of home to her sister Kathleen, away at school; a note to the haberdasher specifying a precise colour and quality of yarn; or a diary entry. The matter of what she was writing seemed to T less important at that moment than the sense of her not being entirely alone in the act. She pictured a figure behind her and so, according to the logic of perspective, behind *her*, in the doorway, watching. Ill-defined but definite enough to catch the hairs of the nape. There was always that feeling when she thought of Annie, a pressure from just outside the frame. And she wondered if, in fact, it wasn't so much that one of Annie's ears was turned to the page as that the other was listening, always, for the step almost beside her in the hall.

¶ *It is the end of my first day here. The sun has almost set and, although I have a lamp, I think it better to wash and ready myself for bed before true darkness falls. I have a horror of extinguishing the light and being surrounded in all directions by black that makes everything disappear, and being swallowed by it as if by freshly turned soil. There was only the thinnest trim of moon last night, tonight there will be none. In any case I am as tired as ever. Dear Bessie has arranged things so that I am quite comfortable, with a high bed and abundant covers and cushions – she has even taken some from the drawing room which I expect Mother will not be pleased to discover. Emmeline telephoned – the line Father put in is a God send – to say she will send over the quilt we finished last Christmas. Even without, I am warm, though the air is sharp and there was frost on the ground this morning. The last of the year, Margaret said to Bessie who said to me, and which I can now say to you alone. Mother says she will bring my scrapbooks over tomorrow. I miss my piano already. And dear Charlie, of course, even though he mocked my voice the other night – to ask for Mendelssohn's 'Song Without Words', really! I know he was only trying to make light of things, and I did laugh, but it wounded me more than I could say.*

IV.

It couldn't have been long between the first signs of illness and the decision to isolate Annie from the rest of the family, up there on the hill behind the house. The hoarse throat, the cough, the random stabbing pain between the shoulder blades, the loss of appetite and constant thirst; the ethereal glitter on her skin.

T had familiarized herself with the symptoms and knew that, by the early 1900s, contagion theory had advanced enough for people to know that if they were in close, sustained proximity with a tuberculous person it was likely they would be 'touched' by an angel of death. But since no adequate methods of diagnosis had been established, what were considered early signs, including the infamous spot of blood ejected onto a handkerchief, were in fact usually proof of an advanced, terminal case. To further complicate matters, T read, the disease changed its character down the centuries and its calling cards – breathlessness, coughing, dizziness, anaemia, lethargy, fevers and night sweats, headaches, insomnia and 'nervous decline' – were always liable to be missed or misidentified as any number of other conditions, especially in women, for whom hysteria remained an easy catch-all.

The word 'hysteria' triggered a memory of her battered edition of Foucault's *The History of Sexuality*, with a detail on its cover from André Brouillet's famous painting, *Une leçon clinique à la Salpêtrière*, in which the celebrity neurologist Jean-Martin Charcot exhibited for an audience of male students his latest attractive young hysteric. It was painted around the time of Annie's birth, T noted, and showed a woman mid swoon, head thrown back, decolleté exposed. As Charcot's assistant held her up, her hand seemed to curl into a fist behind her.

She had not remembered that detail of the fist, actually, but saw it as soon as she lifted the book from the shelf, instinctively smoothing her hand over its cover as if it were coated in thick dust, as all important tomes must be. She thought about the photography studio that Charcot had set up at the clinic to document these women whom he had the power to observe at any time he wished, day or night, from every angle and in various stages of undress. She thought about how, while they slipped from consciousness, he had captured their bodies in images he passed over to other men to compile, caption and circulate in a best-selling book, which was consumed – the word couldn't be bettered – by still more male eyes. Turning the pages, these men read a story of medical progress, of flawed female minds and one remarkable man who could cure them. And the women took it in too.

Every illness, real or otherwise, found itself drawn onto the tracks of narrative, T thought, freighted with expectations about aetiology and symptoms and remedy, from which it deviated only with tremendous will and difficulty. And the route was often not the same for women as for men. Hysteria among men, for instance, was rare, according to Charcot, and generally the result of extreme trauma; they had not the in-built weakness of women.

Tuberculosis was interpreted along similar lines, T saw, fault – genetic, moral or both – being a favourite crutch of medical ignorance. Depending on where in the body it manifested, whether the brain, larynx, bones, kidneys, lymph nodes, pleura, spine or, most commonly, lungs, it went by a different name: consumption, scrofula, white light, *mal de vivre*, the robber of youth, or the 'Romantic Disease', so named for Keats and the countless other bright stars who seemed to translate fever into flights of lucid beauty. She read about King's Evil (cured, they said, by the monarch's charmed kiss) and the White Plague, which matched clinical observation (the pallor of the victims and the white swellings on the surface of an infected organ) with biblical judgement. As if to negate the protean nature of the threat, doctors used the ancient Greek name *phthisis*, 'wasting', far longer than seemed reasonable for a word so difficult to pronounce in a rush. A word so easy to mishear in a whisper as 'syphilis', she thought, one of many shameful conditions with which tuberculosis was often conflated. Long after 1882, when the bacterial cause of tuberculosis was identified, assumptions continued to be made about the predisposition of certain 'types', about careless living and inferior constitutions, about asking for what came to you.

T sank deep into medical history. She would return to bed after dropping A at nursery and lie there for hours, propped up on pillows, the window open, to read about a disease that had been isolated in the bones of Neolithic men and dogged the ancient Egyptians. Only in the late 1800s did doctors begin to understand what they were up against: having stamped on the spit of a tuberculous person as if it were an insect, ground it into the floor with the heel of the boot, and dried and refreshed it multiple times, they found the sample still potent enough to kill. Tuberculosis lived on in victims' tissues long after death, she learnt, survived for months in dust particles in the dark corners of a room, and was carried in asymptomatic 'sleeping' form – right then, now – by about a quarter of the global population. She studied charts that showed its growing resistance to antibiotics, saw that it had recently reemerged as the world's leading infectious killer. And one day, in a crowded café, she looked up from her laptop and wondered if she was in its presence, or if it was already in her.

She thought often of Susan Sontag's essay on the need to liberate ourselves from punitive or sentimental fictions surrounding sickness. In particular, Sontag lamented how the extraordinary susceptibility of the lungs had caused tuberculosis to be seen incorrectly as a one-organ disease and that, because the organ was concerned with breath, and so, in the collective imagination, with life itself, tuberculosis had become aligned with the essence or spirit of a person. 'A disease of the lungs is, metaphorically, a disease of the soul,' she said, as opposed to cancer, which, striking the colon, rectum, breast, bladder, stomach, cervix, prostate, testicles, was all too bodily, embarrassingly so.

Re-reading the essay for the first time in years, T was struck by Sontag's detachment, by the emotional control that prevented her from divulging that only three years earlier cancer had spread from her breasts to the lymph system. The same reserve meant that at no point in eighty-odd pages did she mention that, in 1938, when she was five and so old enough to remember, her father had died of pulmonary tuberculosis while working in China. That her mother, in China too, didn't say a word about it to the children back in New York for months; that when she did, she didn't name the killer because even then a tuberculous death was liable to be read as subtext for tawdry living, poverty and poor hygiene, for a corrupt soul, for Irish, Jewish or other lowly origins. For blame. Even the death certificate draws a veil. Soon after finding out, Sontag had her first asthma attack, a coincidence T found unreasonably compelling.

She thought about the mother's careful suppression of the truth about the death, of her refusal to allow tuberculosis to touch the story of her own life, and asked herself whether Sontag, writing on the fortieth anniversary of the death, hadn't done something similar herself. Not out of shame, but out of a sense that the personal, let alone emotional, life would threaten or degrade the important intellectual work of the essay.

Because of stigma, T read, most patients failed to seek medical help until one of their lungs was wrecked and the prospect of recovery was slim to none. In the first decade of the 1900s, when Annie had fallen ill – even that formulation seemed to suggest responsibility, a clumsy placing of the feet – her family would have bristled at the word 'consumption', but 'Tuberculosis' wasn't widespread enough outside of medical circles to replace it. Possibly they didn't name it at all, accepting its presence and dropping into the 'shy, evasive, glassy-eyed manner of speech' with which Kafka, some years later, himself in the advanced stages of the disease, was confronted.

Would Annie have understood what was happening to her? T wondered. Did anyone explain it to her, or, at eighteen, was she worldly enough to know for herself? Did she feel – was she made to feel – culpable for her own misfortune? Did she piece together an incomplete version of things, drawing in scraps by or about Keats and Shelley and the Brontës, the last of whom, Charlotte, had died quite recently and not so far away, just on the other side of the moors. Annie would surely have read of the weariness, fever and fret, of the 'leaden-eyed despairs' and the dull, perplexed brain, and would have known what was to come next: that 'youth grows pale, and spectre-thin, and dies'. Probably she had recited Keats's lines by heart, never suspecting them as a primer for her own end.

One afternoon, T spent a few hours researching sanatoriums, plotting them on a map in relation to the manor house, and looking up pictures of the institutions, which ranged from rudimentary and unheated wooden huts to bright white health palaces on the coast, with spacious dining and drawing rooms, acres of private land and miniature golf courses. She wondered if the family – though, really, it would have been Charles's decision alone – had considered sending Annie to be treated in such a place, or removing her from the cold, damp winds to warmer climes abroad, where it was believed the sun could slow the disease's progress. Because if your daughter were ill, she thought, you would seek the finest professional care you could afford, and this family could afford a great deal.

She couldn't have said why she dismissed the notion; only that something about Charles, something she had felt since the first time she heard the story about a young woman confined, suggested that he would have wanted to keep Annie close, where he could see her, to treat her himself. He was a medical man, after all, educated and confident, with knowledge so specialized his words must have appeared foreign to those around him (often they were). And he was experienced, too, no doubt, for the sooty, overcrowded city he had left behind not so long ago would have brought hundreds of tuberculous cases to his attention (perhaps, she thought, the family moved to be rid of them). With the faceless many, though, he could never have guaranteed obedience to a treatment plan, and this must have been frustrating for a man conditioned for exactitude. He could only ever take the word of his patients – or is it clients? – that they swallowed the correct dose of cod liver oil twice daily, rested after meals, walked miles each day to air the lungs (like an old rug, he thought, the chest could take a good beating). And, anyway, both parties knew rest was not an option when there were so many jobs to do and mouths to feed. So, mostly, they died and there was no satisfaction for Charles in that.

With Annie came a chance to test his learning and theories, then, and T imagined him throwing himself into the challenge, his ambition galvanized, perhaps, by a secret suspicion that it might in fact have been he who let the white light in in the first place. The stakes could not have been higher than his own child's life.

So, she set him there in her mind, on the hill above the village, as the labourers brought his ideas brick-by-brick to reality, and had him slap his palms against his thighs, to a music hall rhythm, in nervous anticipation. If love or doubt or fear were with him then, they did not trouble the scene.

And the more she thought along those lines, the more that tower of white stone and glass became what people who knew nothing at all of the story had always told her it was: a folly, a monument to great vanity and conceit.

V.

A camera slid slowly down a row of eleven chalk-white ribs, gently curved like mandolin blades, scrubbed of all organic matter and arranged concentrically against a perfect black background.

She was watching a silent film from the 1920s in which a young woman was about to have the ribs on one side of her chest extracted by a surgeon. T had been shown X-rays that proved the advanced state of the illness: this was chronic fibroid tuberculosis, which meant that the walls of the lungs, usually fine and flexible, had thickened and stiffened like dried papier-mâché. There were multiple cavities, formed by abscesses which carved out airy, necrotic pockets of tissue in which the bacteria thrived. No amount of rest, not even in a superior sanatorium with golf and dinner-dances, could have abated so advanced a case. She would have lost her appetite almost entirely by now, that woman, ironically developing 'air hunger', an insatiable sense of breath-starvation caused by the calcification of the chest. Probably she had grown used to the sight of blood in her handkerchief. The X-rayed ribs looked wispy, T thought, as if the bones were turning to smoke before her very eyes, a disappearing act that had likely begun in childhood.

Another set of X-rays showed the same woman post-operation, with a caption pronouncing 'Complete Thoracoplasty Collapse of the Left Side', corroborated by an image in which half of her chest was opaque, milky. The harsh wheezes, the gurgles and dull pops, creaks, growls, grating, scratching, the *rhonchi*, *râles*, rattles and other irregularities of breath that had been companion noises for most of the woman's life – a whole language for the physician to translate back to her – had been silenced.

She was, in a way, alive and dead at the same time, T thought, the left side having been smothered to give the right a fighting chance.

The film cut back to the operating theatre and T held her breath.

'Patient reaches the operating room in complete relaxation induced by preoperative administration of six grains of Sodium Amytal and one-fourth grain of morphine.' She paused the film, opened a tab on her laptop and typed in 'Sodium Amytal'. She read that soon after synthesis it came to be valued less for its sedative powers than for the so-called truth-telling trances it triggered in subjects whose memories were said to flourish and flow freely under its influence. General anaesthesia was not used, so the patient remained conscious, albeit sedated, throughout. T remembered having her wisdom teeth removed; how no amount of local anaesthetic could have dimmed her awareness of the dentist's tools in her mouth, his hands shaking with exertion, the way he fell back into his chair with every extraction.

A thick needle jabbed novocaine into the tissue behind the woman's left shoulder blade, leaving evenly spaced lumps, like garlic cloves under chicken skin. T watched as the surgeon easefully joined these to make his first incision, cutting through the skin and 'other superficial structures', each slice of the knife bringing a deeper parting of glistening flesh. In the film's colourless world, still T registered yellow-whites, watery pinks, such hectic reds. As the trapezius and rhomboid muscles were divided (so a caption said), six hands dabbed and pulled and clamped, tugged and cut and ripped, until the ribs were finally exposed. For a brief moment, all hands and tools withdrew to admire a masterpiece: the cavity sagged as if releasing a sigh.

41

White cloth and more novocaine were plugged straight into the wound and gauze packed beneath the ribs, the surgeon using some kind of chisel to prise each up a little further, to be flush with the lip of the cavity. The fifth, fourth and third ribs were removed, in that order, clipped at both ends just out of sight, with shears like those she had seen used in kitchens, to spatchcock a bird. Then commenced 'The Attack of the Second and Third Ribs', like a battle waged for sovereignty along a wild frontier.

T nodded, as if to show an imaginary observer she was no rookie. She had done her homework and knew that, while eleven of a person's total twelve ribs per side might be removed in a single thoracoplasty, good practice dictated that the first rib be left in place for cosmetic reasons, especially in women, to reduce deformity and preserve as much as possible the delicate architecture of the neck and shoulder. This was according to a particular type of thoracoplasty, pioneered at the time by a surgeon who dedicated himself to improving a lifesaving procedure that had been around in far cruder forms for some decades. Hundreds of students had learnt John Alexander's method and, while antibiotics had replaced the need for the operation in most places, even now it remained in use in faraway countries, where drug resistance and systemic chaos conspired to reverse the advance of medical time. She wondered if that film was also a vision of the future.

As the camera panned out to show the operating surgeon's face, she thought it must be Alexander's disciple she was looking at, if not the great man himself. It seemed possible in the heat of the moment. She paused the film and enlarged the screen to scrutinize the large nose and bespectacled eyes under neat brows, framed by the sterile white of a surgical mask and cap. She opened another tab and started to search. Alexander suffered from tuberculosis himself, she read, of the pleura, spine and kidneys, for most of his adult life; several obituaries said it recurred periodically, sometimes forcing him to rest in a remote sanatorium hundreds of miles from his home. He died in the 1950s, at the age of sixty-three, by which point antibiotic treatment had become established, and she wondered if he felt sorrow or relief at the thought of never pruning another rib. In a memorial article she learnt of his love of hunting and of Thanksgiving dinners thrown for staff and family, with a turkey carved expertly by his hand.

Returning to the film, T felt guilt; she had forgotten all about the woman on the table, with her chest open to the world and six busy hands inside her. She watched with renewed attention as they removed the last of the five ribs and completed the multi-layered process of unclamping and suturing 'with continuous silk', which made it sound almost luxurious. She, the patient, a bundle of white sheets as heavy and still as a toppled sculpture, was then wheeled on a gurney from one room to a second, where three nurses moved her clumsily into a convalescent bed. A rough splice in the film suggested that more than one attempt was made. An embarrassed look flickered across the face of one of the nurses, T thought, and the patient's eyes widened for a split second and her mouth opened as if in shock, then firmly closed.

In the next scene she blinked against the light and her lips moved again, more than once, and there was definite speech this time: uninhibited truth escaping, only to be failed by soundless technology. What had she said? Whose name did she call? Perhaps she only asked for a glass of water. A nurse stood at the head of the bed with one hand on the pillow, near but not touching. She did not appear to respond, although her face was out of view so T couldn't be sure. She primped the bedding in a studied display of attention, careful not to obscure the camera's view with her own body.

The final few minutes of the film were taken up with a parade, a 'Demonstration of Operated Patients Showing Absence of Marked Deformity'. A woman seen from behind, her back naked, sat on a stool and raised her arms above her head, hands just out of view, so that T couldn't help but imagine her about to bring down an axe. She had two neat, parallel scars across the right shoulder blade, like the trainlines on an old map. A second woman perched in the same position while the doctor's hand wandered across her smooth skin, gently stroking from right to left, as if feeling the weave of a fine silk rug. (T felt her own muscles tense between the shoulder blades, around the spot where, as a child, she was convinced wings would sprout if only she imagined hard enough.) A third woman, with tight finger-waves across her brow, spun slowly on the stool giving a 360° view of her torso. Her breasts were secured by a strapless hospital gown, giving her the air of a dishevelled Grecian goddess. She bit her lip and giggled as she rotated, and although, or because, she felt eyes on her, she kept her own to the floor. Another looked straight into the lens, laughing as she turned on her axis, so that T hardly noticed the scars. The last of them danced down an imaginary catwalk and pivoted on her heel before giving the camera a coquettish smile and slipping away forever.

T observed the procession of images with a certain detachment, judging each woman on the quality of her eyes, skin, hair and general demeanour. Just two men, one in his fifties, the other in his twenties, completed the data set – that's what you'd call it, I guess – and it troubled her in a misty, open-ended sort of way. She rewound,

44

paused, zoomed in on the women, peering deep into the film's pores. It was like a casting reel for the role of Annie, she thought, although it was more than a decade out of time and an ocean away. There were eleven women in all, some remarkably unblemished, while the contorted backs and slack shoulders of others contradicted the captionist's confidence. In each case, X-ray images hovered in the background like apparitions of the people they once were.

At the end, a final caption – 'Well on the way to recovery' – announced a group scene in which about two dozen former patients posed for a photograph in Sunday hats and fur-trimmed coats. They huddled close together, linked arms; some stood behind others who sat or crouched on the lawns outside the sanatorium, catching up on life. The trees around about were bare, their branches unignorably bronchiole-like. Once the photograph was taken, the women walked towards the camera, smiling and zhuzhing their hair, sashaying, sauntering, full of hope where once their lungs had rattled loneliness and death like two dice in cup.

But T didn't really see those people anymore. Instead, she saw scars, faded but ever-present, like the marks left by ivy pulled from a painted wall; torsos twisted like wrung-out towels; brittle lungs like coral prised from a reef. She pictured them all, displayed with innumerable other trophies in the eternally touring global exhibit of medical progress. And their ribs, like so many silver collars set in velvet.

¶ *I've run out of books and am reading the same things over and over. Mother says she will bring me something new to read tomorrow. She goes to town every Wednesday, market day, but it seems an eternity between. Emmeline says she will send me* The Blue Lagoon, *just as soon as she has finished reading it herself for the second or third time – she says she has never 'experienced' anything half as good. That is her word, by the way, so I suspect some of the book's power over her lies in the heroine sharing her name, for it must be strange and compelling to read of yourself on such wild adventures in distant lands when you are sitting in an armchair in a dull part of the world, where nothing much ever happens. Charlie says it's a silly book, which only a child would be taken in by. But as Father says I am not to overdo my reading it may be just the thing. It took days of pleading for him to let me bring the Shelleys, Mary and Percy (for I'd never separate them). In the end he stopped taking the telephone, and it was Charlie who persuaded him I don't know how. 'You mustn't excite yourself.' If I had a penny for every time Father has said those words I should be set up quite nicely in one of those magical Swiss sanatoriums where the princesses and maharajas go, instead of here stewing in cod liver oil and iodine. Charlie says Father closes himself in his study for hours on end, and reads medical papers even at the table so that no one can talk without incurring his wrath. He's a regular mad professor, he said. But wouldn't that make me his monster.*

VI

What treatments had they tried before resorting to the tower's walls; panaceas for Annie and prophylactics for themselves? Charles had probably heard about developments in the field of thoracoplasty, that surgeons were making such leaps, but if he had informed himself and asked around, he would only have been told the procedure was experimental and magnificently risky, not to be attempted outside of the most elite, specialist institutions. The timing of Annie's plight was part of its peculiar tragedy, T thought: she lived and died in a hinterland, between the ancient and obscure cures of folklore and the radiant advances of medical science, between ass milk and antibiotics.

T imagined a household divided between the served and the serving, an upstairs-downstairs in which the drawing room's stories of medical triumph, gleaned from the *Lancet* and other specialized sources, co-existed with the cook's dramatic account of her nephew's friend's brother, who was cured by digging out the roots of a black elder tree, when the moon was waning before dawn, hanging them around his neck for twenty-four hours, then flinging them into a fast-running river – straight into the river, she said, just downstream of us here – while reciting the Lord's Prayer several times. (Seven or nine, the cook couldn't recall, the main thing was that it be an odd number.)

Days were passed in the library, T pulling out paper after paper on folklore remedies. She pondered sixteenth-century astrological charts that claimed that if you were born with the moon in the fourth house, in conjunction with Mars or Saturn, you were likely to develop 'paines or diseases in the Lunges'. (She made a note to check for

A; her own paines were known to her already.) She read of a Polynesian belief, apparently still alive in the 1930s, according to which the demon Mumu was responsible for afflicting the chest with tuberculosis, so the physician, swinging a spear over his patient's head, cried 'Oh! Mumu, Oh! Mumu! I am about to spear thee.' The woman from the hospital film, with her hands above her head, returned to T; she replaced her axe with a spear. And how close was Mumu to *mamma*, she thought, the cry of a scared child.

She had come across an article by the physician and folklorist John Davy Rolleston in which he described a treatment, allegedly in use in parts of Austria around the time of Annie's illness, where a living trout was strapped to the sufferer's chest and left to die and decay. In some places, he said, 'a goldfish is employed, being given three days to waste away. If this does not happen it is a poor look out for the patient.' She was reminded of the bright orange fortune-telling 'fish' that came in cheap Christmas crackers and which, placed on the palm of the hand, promised to diagnose you through the contortions of its own body, a supreme act of empathy: if it moved its head, you were jealous, but if its tail waved at the same time, you were in love; if it flipped over, you were false, which seemed to her, as a child, a curious thing to be. Her family would pass it around the table, gripped by the miracle, or, she realized later, pretending. She remembered an occasion, she must have been about eight, where it lay in her hand without a twitch: 'You're dead!' her sister shouted, and for a moment, she thought she might be.

Rolleston listed the animals people turned to in the hope of a cure, alphabetically but not exhaustively: adder, ass, badger, blackbird, cat, clam, cock, cod, cow (milk, horn, dung), crab, crayfish, crocodile, crow, deer, dog, fox (lung, dung), frog, goat, hen, herring, horse (dung), lamprey, lizard, louse, marmoset, mullet, ox (bone marrow), oyster, periwinkle, pig (dung), rabbit (dung), seal, sheep, shrimp, slug, snail, spider, swallow, turkey, turtle, wolf and worm. She found a poster from 1920 in a medical archive in which a giant, fanged black spider, representing tuberculosis, pulled the bodies of countless emaciated men, women and children into her web. (The *her* was automatic; spiders are always *she*, even when they are not.) She puzzled over the idea of the spider as both illness and cure, on the side of the aggressor and of the victim, and thought that if she concentrated, she might hit on a way of reconciling the opposites, a narrative logic in which everything clicked into place. It isn't quite true what they say, about each poison containing its own antidote.

In most cases, the flesh of Rolleston's animals was consumed, raw or cooked, or the fat melted down and worked into a paste and spread across the chest. Plants, whose remedies were even more numerous than those drawn from animals, were often added, ranging from the acorn to the yarrow, through marigold, marrubium, marsh mallow, mistletoe and mugwort. One especially sophisticated recipe called for a swallow's nest cooked with milk, honey, butter and a little saffron, then wrapped in a muslin and applied warm to the patient's chest; another, where consumption was caused by 'sexual excess', for the testes of a fox or chicken to be hung about the torso. Health by humiliation. Sheep and cows were prized, Rolleston explained, for their breath, curative if inhaled, so that the patient was made to sleep on a bed in the middle of a field, in a barn or butcher's shop. The *patient*. She circled the word. No matter how fabulous the course of action, Rolleston remained wedded to this term so caught up in

**ITALIANI, AIVTATE LA CROCE ROSSA
NELL'ASSISTENZA AI TVBERCOLOSI**

the corridors of medicine, tangled up with stethoscope and scale. At first, she thought him wry and ironic; then she appreciated his simple correctness, medical use having followed the general understanding of a person who persevered through pain, as a witness to the fate of their own body. Patience incarnate, with the scars to prove it.

How many of these oils, distillates and powders had found their way into the pills and ointments of Annie's day, she wondered. There were few restrictions on the making and selling of 'medicine', and no obligation to list ingredients. Advertisements for miracle cures were rife and for those looking to be convinced that all was not lost, quite irresistible. In the depths of a medical museum, T found advertisements full of persuasion and promise, especially in magazines destined for monied and socially aspirant women, as Annie and her fur-swaddled sisters were. Money bought kinds of hope that the poor could hardly imagine, as they stirred blood and dung with conviction.

One day, in some archive or other, she found a notice of 1900 for 'Dr Williams' Pink Pills for Pale People', which, in bold red type on pastel-pink paper, schooled prospective clients in 'Facts about the Old Century and the New':

> The greatest advances in the last part of the Old Century have been those in the Science of Medicine. The Old Medicine – which is still the Ordinary Medicine in general use – aimed at curing the SYMPTOMS of disease.... The New Medical Science dates from the discovery of Dr Williams' Pink Pills.

And so, just like that, the scene was set for a tale of antagonism, T thought, between Old and New, the Ordinary and 'the very ripest achievement of Advanced Medical

Science' – which by treating 'the CAUSES of the Disease' made symptoms vanish 'as if by magic'. Few readers, even those who professed themselves firmly on the side of the Scientific, could entirely resist a hint of the supernatural.

The patent for Pink Pills had been bought some years earlier, T discovered, by George Taylor Fulford, a Canadian farmer's son turned entrepreneur, who capitalized on cheap postage, the expansion of the railways and the unprecedented advertising opportunity brought by the new mass media. There was great cleverness in the marketing, she conceded, which he entrusted to a former newspaper editor: current-affairs style 'reports' and the stories of 'cured' members of the public formed the thrust of the campaigns, designed to appeal to the average person's belief in the honesty of other people just like them. A frank and level-headed address – 'Write to us and tell us your Symptoms.... We will not sell pills except where we think they will cure' – was matched by lines designed to milk hope from even the most wretched: 'Do not be afraid to write because Doctors have failed to cure you, or because you have been told you are incurable. Dr Williams' Pink Pills are not like other medicine. They have cured thousands of cases where other medicines failed.'

In the first decade of the twentieth century, T read, the company's international advertising budget – because soon there were branches in major global cities – surpassed a million dollars, about $32 million in today's terms. The newspapers chose not to explore the dubiousness of this most significant client – and, anyway, the pills, iron-rich, *did* seem to work in some cases, such as anaemia, so who could say, definitively, that they were good for nothing? We use the same word, 'story', to describe a verifiable matter of fact, a self-proclaimed work of the imagination, and the brazen lie. Did we never foresee a problem?

The pills were evidently popular because Dr Williams felt the need to run another kind of advert, this time under the banner 'WARNINGS for 1900'. The primary antagonist was now 'Substitutes', which were 'Ordinary Medicine' dressed up to look like Dr Williams' Pink Pills. But,

> Be Warned! Do not believe anything that is told you about a Substitute being "as good".... You will do well to avoid anyone who tries to deceive you in this way.... The dealer is trying to cheat you.

She felt herself on familiar ground, encircled by wolves dressed as benevolent old ladies, their claws and teeth barely concealed, and knew it would not do to leave the reader in a state of hopeless fear at the story's end. Hopeful fear was the only productive kind, the lucrative kind. A 'Handy List of Diseases that *have been cured* by Dr Williams' Pink Pills' was appended, by turns specific and as vague as happy-ever-after:

> Paralysis, Locomotor Ataxy, Spinal Disease, Anaemia, Pale and Sallow Complexion, Palpitation of the Heart, Consumption and "Decline", General Debility, Sleeplessness, St. Vitus' Dance, Rickets, Loss of Vital Forces, Rheumatism, Sciatica, Biliousness, Pimples, Eczema and Skin Disorders, Neuralgia, Nervous Headache, Sick Headache and Indigestion, Chronic Liver Complaint, After-effects of Influenza, Scrofula, Kidney Diseases; And the following Disorders of Women: Suppression or Excess of the Menses, Hysteria, Change of Life, Leucorrhoea ("Whites").

Finally, the reader was urged to act: 'Dr Williams' Pink Pills for Pale People can be obtained at most Chemists' Shops and Drug Stores; but in case of doubt' – and who, she thought, would not doubt their own judgement now? – 'it is better to send (enclosing the price: 2/9 for one box, or 13/9 for six boxes) to DR WILLIAMS' MEDICINE CO.' An address was given which she recognized as just around the corner from somewhere she used to work, and after all the mystification this seemed ridiculous, as if a line had been crossed and a fairy tale forced into a lowly kind of real-world service.

You swallow a story as you swallow a pill, and she wondered how many Annie and her family swallowed. 'Dr Williams' Pink Pills for Pale People can be obtained at most Chemists' Shops and Drug Stores' – so had Charles stocked them, too? Had he brought them home to try? And how about Congreve's Balsamic Elixir, a bright red herbal blend of vegetable matter and sulphuric acid, with a touch of Tolu and Peru balsam, Virginia prune, a sedative, and copious quantities of sugar, cochineal and alcohol; or Dr Derk P. Yonkerman's regime combining 'self-control' and the 'wonderful specific, discovered after twenty years of ceaseless research, Tuberculozyne', which boasted, Yonkerman claimed, 'miraculous healing powers ... also in far-advanced and seemingly hopeless cases'; or 'Crimson Cross Fever Powder for the Cure of Consumption', whose powers presumably lay in alliteration; or 'Lung Germaine', with its giddy notice that 'initially the germs being torn mercilessly from their lodgements may induce a feeling of weakness ... *but this is the turning point!*'

Sugar, alcohol, sedative, hope; it was difficult to imagine a more deliciously addictive concoction. She was reminded of the crowded window displays of the pharmacies where she grew up, abroad, which advertised competing weight-loss 'treatments', all 'natural', all 'herbal', all extraordinary. Inside, a pharmacist in a starched white lab coat would talk the patient through the options; 'classic' flavours – chocolate, strawberry, vanilla – were also available, for the less mature palate. Decades later, walking around her hometown with her husband, he pointed out how those pharmacies seemed to have preserved a mask of clinical authority vanished from other pharmacies in other places; whenever he went in, he said, he couldn't help but feel reassured, in the hands of professionals. She nodded, remembering girls she went to school with, who before puberty had run its course were taking pills and supplements bought for them by their mothers or, with pocket money, for themselves. She thought about how envious she had been, charmed by the possibility contained in those colourful sachets of powder, and remembered the creams they had enthusiastically shared with her, for unwanted hair, orange-peel skin, spider veins and countless other imperfections no child has ever had.

She had always had it in her, that hunger for the quick fix, for a fairy tale transformation, for the just about believable unbelievable. Even now, as she read articles about the treatment of tuberculosis and searched the internet for traces of Annie, she was distracted by pop-up adverts that proclaimed to have discovered 'Three simple and AMAZING cures' for cellulite or insomnia or wrinkles. Her eye lingered a little longer than it should. But she didn't click the link. She never did. Partly in fear that her computer would be compromised by some invisible virus; partly in fear that her mind would be compromised, or already was and all that remained was to admit it. Then find the cure.

¶ *I wish someone could tell me what occurs in the mind in the night when the body sleeps. On waking it is as though a witch, sometimes kind, sometimes wicked, has sat by the pillow for hours and with her long, carved ladle stirred up the potion, spooning up thoughts and memories from below to the surface, dragging others down to the depths for some other time. What seemed of vital importance at bedtime is turned over for something I didn't even know was there, trivial or obscure. This morning, I had a head full of exotic birds, my first thoughts inexplicably taking up the thread of something I read – but so many years ago! – in one of Father's magazines, as if I had been dwelling on it for hours before waking. It will sound mad, but I was thinking of these great crested parrots, extinct for God knows how long and only discovered by their remains – bits of a long, curved beak dug up from a bog somewhere on the other side of the world. And I was thinking of the plates they had in that magazine, to illustrate the article, showing the parrot in various shades of green and yellow with its curious frontal crest just above that hook of a beak, and its full breast and funny short wings like a handless pair of child's mittens. They say they were flightless, their wings purely for show, which is why they were hunted into oblivion. But what I was thinking about, the thought that actually woke me up with a jolt, was that nobody could say what colour they were, those dear departed birds. No one could ever truly, with their hand on their heart, say for sure that they were not red or blue or pink, or any other colour I should wish them to have been.*

VII

Some months later T sat in the kitchen after lunch, contemplating a series of photographs of a young woman, swiping left and right on her phone. Everyone was saying that day would be the summer's last, that the heat would give way to autumn chill tomorrow, so T had the doors wide open into the garden. The wolf cooked himself on the flagstones outside, his ears twitching at occasional birdsong. The basement kitchen was cool, slightly damp, so flies came seeking respite. A bluebottle landed on her hand, suspended over the keyboard as she waited for a word to come to her. It didn't come, and the fly, impatient, relocated to a teaspoon on the table, where it probed a shallow pool of milky coffee.

The woman in the photographs wore a plush velvet coat with a pussy-bow and fur collar, a wide-brimmed hat crowned with ostrich feathers, and her eyes gave away nothing, no expression whatsoever. In another, she was dressed as a Ukrainian peasant girl, in a thick cotton blouse with billowing sleeves. She was bareheaded, hair pulled back and centre-parted to show a full-moon face, her eyes – with unmistakable wryness now – fixed on the lens. Her lips were slightly parted, as if the photographer had surprised her just as she began to say something. She was standing in a studio, a soft, painted landscape on the silkscreen behind her, her naked feet planted on what appeared to be a mixture of soil and decaying leaves, imported, T supposed, for authenticity. It was difficult to make out; it could have been lush, thick-pile carpet.

She flicked through other photographs – here she had a dog, there a mandolin or a strange hat, like a napkin dropped from the sky – to one which showed her standing in a white, Grecian style off-the-shoulder dress, her hair twisted into a mound of unreal curls. Her left hand rested on the back of a chair, while the other cupped her chin as she gazed in the opposite direction, supported by an elbow propped on an ornate plinth. I am a sculpture, she seemed to be saying; I am the work of art.

How T had ended up there, considering this woman's image at her leisure, she couldn't have told you, except that it was apparently impossible to research the tuberculous experience without coming across the artist Marie Bashkirtseff. The algorithms had led her there; she had only followed.

An émigré from the Russian Empire, born between Kyiv and Kharkiv in present-day Ukraine, Bashkirtseff had burnt out in Paris on 31 October 1884, just shy of her twenty-sixth birthday. Or her twenty-fourth, depending on who was talking. She was a genius or a sham, formidable or pathetic. Russian or Ukrainian – they would make that choice for her, too. Her fame rested on a diary kept from a young age until her final days, which chronicled in suffocating detail the every thought, emotion and desire of an exuberant girl, then increasingly ill woman, who railed against the injustice of a patriarchal society that would not grant her what she wanted above all else: to be known and, through that, she thought, to be free.

The journal was published in a heavily redacted and reconfigured edition shortly after her death, T read, by her mother and André Theuriet, a novelist friend, who also offered a sickly-sweet epitaph for an extravagant mausoleum, a recreation of the artist's studio, complete with marble busts, books, canvases and a divan, in the Cimetière de Passy. The pair had agreed that, for the sake of the story – that is, to amplify its effect – they would shave off two years from the woman's age. The diary became a sensation and within weeks of

publication hundreds of thousands of copies had been sold. Newspapers cited a 'Bashkirtseff Boom'. In archives T read reviews and features in which opinion split between those who trusted it as a document of the 'feminine' experience and those who thought Bashkirtseff's confidences, particularly descriptions of flirtations and trysts, fabricated and vulgar without virtue.

Admirers flocked to Bashkirtseff's home in Paris's seventeenth arrondissement to experience for themselves rooms that had once contained a wild and colourful spirit, and the mother received each pilgrim gladly, showing them around, pointing out books discarded half-read on a bedside table or a shawl draped over the back of a chair, as if Marie had just come in from a stroll. As if, in fact, as soon as she had breathed her last, the whole place had been suspended in time by the flash of a photographer's bulb, trapping the living and breathing inside a one-dimensional world.

Memoirs followed by those who knew the artist, or claimed to have, in which T noted an emphasis on heavy ermine furs, blouses à la Vandyke, white satin slippers. Translations of the journal came thick and fast, among them an English translation by a poet and social campaigner, Mathilde Blind, who had been an early visitor to the Bashkirtseff residence. The name was vaguely familiar to T from an article she had once read about a famous artist and his wife, a love triangle, a media storm; she knew nothing of her work or achievements.

At her laptop in the kitchen, T read Blind's introduction to her 1890 translation and was surprised – disappointed, I suppose – by the gushy tone, by the fact that Blind appeared to have unquestioningly accepted the mother's account of her daughter, adjusted age and all, admiring how her 'pious love' had so perfectly preserved the atmosphere of rooms in which Marie had spent her final years 'in a kind of artistic delirium.'

Blind's eye was sensitive to things that showed us the woman: the 'valuable editions of Greek and Roman classics in orderly rows along the shelves'; Italian, French, German, English and Russian literature; 'a striking photograph of Émile Zola, for whom this artist entertained so pronounced an admiration' hung near the desk at which she wrote her diary and letters. Marie, too, was a naturalist of the highest order, T read, who,

> asks to be face to face with actual facts, instead of dealing with figments of the fancy; to present the "living Life" through the medium of colour as she so triumphantly managed to convey it through that of words.... Not beauty, not invention, not

– here Blind quotes Wordsworth – 'The light that never was on sea or land.'

Blind treated her subject's belongings as she did the words she went on to translate, lifting each up, looking for meanings below and above, seizing the one she found to be truest and considering its position in the whole, as if Bashkirtseff's possessions were grammatical units and her life a sentence (which, in a way, it was). Those rooms contained for Blind 'what seemed to bring Marie Bashkirtseff in the flesh more vividly before me than the books and the furniture, the statues and pictures, and all the rest of it'. She lit on a cupboard full of 'little' shoes: 'house-shoes, dress-shoes, ball-shoes – but what a world of pathos was there not in those bits of leather or satin which had shod those small Cinderella-like feet.'

The fairy tale register, and the talk of little and small, seemed to sit awkwardly alongside Blind's opening lines, in which she described the diary as 'in the nude, breathing and palpitating with life', as 'an education in psychology'. It felt wrong in light of Bashkirtseff's apparently fierce, dedicated naturalism. But T allowed herself to be lulled by Blind as she reached the final months of her heroine's life, when she struggled to paint at all, when what little energy that remained was poured into languid hours spent with her friend and mentor, the painter Jules Bastien-Lepage, who was also dying, of cancer. Blind's sentences rushed into each other, gathering a fluid kind of force, until Marie and Jules were united in a strange wash of *Vogue* feature and Shakespearean tragedy:

> Propped up on cushions the two dying artists lay near each other, finding a supreme consolation in being together to the last. Marie Bashkirtseff, not forgetful of appearances even then, wore a tea-gown of ivory plush with a cloud of soft lace of every shade of white. The artist's grey eyes, "eyes which had beheld Joan of Arc", as she says, dilated with pleasure as he looked at her.

A few days later, on 20 October, Marie made her final journal entry, and eleven days later, on All Hallows Eve, she was dead. 'That is all,' wrote Blind, with the undisguisable relish of the storyteller. 'Shortly before completing her twenty-fourth year, Marie Bashkirtseff had ceased to be, and was followed shortly afterwards by Bastien-Lepage, so that in their death they were not divided.'

T knew it wasn't true, of course, that Bashkirtseff was the less-tragic side of twenty-five, and it seemed fair to assume would have dropped Lepage sooner or later as she had every man before him. 'I look down on men,' she wrote in her diary, 'from such a height that I behave charmingly to them, for it would not do to despise those who are so far below me. I consider them as a cat might a mouse.' But Blind, what had she believed?

Later, T imagined Marie in the photographer's studio again, trying on outfits and tilting her head this way and that, arching her neck and letting the light fall to striking effect, to accentuate the lines of her cheek, collar or breast, to conceal those across her brow. Only now she seemed to see the finest of silk threads emanating from the crown of the head and from both wrists, tugged taut with a master's intent. And those dainty feet were suspended just a hair's breadth above the earth, powerless to move her.

.

After she had read about the diary, she set about reading the thing itself, beginning with a preface added by Bashkirtseff towards the end of her life. In the digital copy she had found for free online, she isolated a passage, using the cursor like a brush to wash it a light watery blue:

> Why tell lies and play a part? Yes, it is clear that I have the wish, if not the hope, of remaining on this earth by whatever means in my power. If I do not die young, I hope to survive as a great artist; but if I do, I will have my Journal published, which cannot fail to be interesting. But as I talk of publicity, this idea of being read has perhaps spoilt, nay, destroyed, the sole merit of such a book? Well, no! To begin with, I wrote for a long time without a thought of being read, and in the next place it is precisely because I hope to be read that I am absolutely sincere. If this book be not the exact, the absolute, the strict truth, it has no right to exist.... Rest assured, therefore, kind reader, that I reveal myself completely, entirely.

You couldn't ask for a more explicit expression of the author's hope, later her mother's, publisher's and translator's, that the book carry on where the life ended. But it was more than that, she thought: Bashkirtseff seemed to want the picture she made of herself in words to replace the woman who had written them: the book as pound of flesh, as transection of the author's abdomen, with its many and varied layers, from smooth skin and firm muscle to marbled fat, indigo bruises, frayed nerves. A kind of reverse transubstantiation; the mess of a body alchemized into paper and ink, wafer-thin and obliquely, intimately satisfying.

One day, T came across an American edition of the diary whose title seemed to capture the spirit of Bashkirtseff's project: *I Am the Most Interesting Book of All.* She searched the diary several times and didn't find the line, although it sounded so much like something Bashkirtseff might have said. (They do her voice too, she thought.) And it struck her then how perfect an illustration Bashkirtseff made of Jean Baudrillard's theory about the representation of a thing taking on a life of its own, leaving the original to dwindle into insignificance as if it had never existed (if it ever had). She almost slapped the table: *This* is what I've been driving at, she thought. Marie Bashkirtseff didn't interest her, the skilful painting and unconventional politics seemed incidental: it was the story she was there for. Or even, the story of the story: a sorry tale of endless reproduction, of aura-less art; of a woman trapped between mirrors, her infinite selves trailing into eternity in both directions. Which is real? Who decides? At what cost?

She knew what she was doing.

Precisely that line came suddenly into her mind, and it shocked her because the words weren't hers; at least, she didn't hear them in her own voice. It was as if they had been crouched inside her – for how long? – like foreign agents waiting for a moment's weakness. She wrote the words down on the back of a receipt and stared for a while, wondering if it was possible to read them in any way other than as disapproval, to add them up and come out with a result that didn't equal unpitying dismissal of a woman who would apparently sell her soul for fame, unpitying dismissal of whatever happened or might yet happen to her. Or to her story, she wasn't sure of the difference anymore.

She knew what she was doing.

T added up the words. It wasn't that Marie Bashkirtseff had put herself out there, salted and spiced, to be torn apart by a reading public hungry for novelty and transgression. That wasn't the thing that scared T. Rather it was that, in doing so, Bashkirtseff had relinquished a hold on her own story, she who had taken such pains to capture it with such *honesty* – that word appeared again and again in the journal, alongside truth and sincerity. And T didn't know which was more tragic: that Bashkirtseff believed those concepts possible, or that she, T, might not.

.

Towards the end of her short life, Bashkirtseff apparently turned against those early character photographs of herself, with the hats and the mandolin. They were contrived, she said, 'false', as if she had drawn a line under such girlish behaviours and was now truth incarnate. As if the two were opposites.

That day in the kitchen, T found another portrait: Bashkirtseff's face in light charcoal on mottled parchment the colour of weak tea, what remained of her loose hair lank and unkempt. Her eyes, half closed, appeared to be melting down her sallow cheeks, towards an almost lipless mouth.

This, she learnt, was Bashkirtseff as sketched by Gustave Courtois in the final days, perhaps hours, of life. She was very small. Not 'small' in the way Blind cast her, petite and pretty; but 'small' in a strictly mathematical sense, in proportion to the pillows and duvet, which rose all around her like clouds. The picture had an academic air, like a study in the tuberculous death, where the body and, by this point, spirit had been all but consumed by disease. No ivory plush or soft lace, no twinkling eyes, no glint of Joan of Arc or Cinderella. The chattering fairies had deserted her, leaving a sepulchral silence.

She didn't encounter this image in a museum archive, I should say, or on any website of historical repute. She had come across it by chance as she searched for more in the playful costume series. She clicked a link and there she was: '*The death of Maria Konstantinovna Bashkirtseva 1858–1884*, 1884, by Gustave Courtois. Available as an art print on canvas, photo paper, watercolor board, uncoated paper or Japanese paper.' She was invited to buy her in the size of her choice, with borders or without, in a glossy, matte or satin finish.

As T pondered the options, although she had no real intention of making a purchase, she was distracted by a persistent buzz coming from the corner of the kitchen, by the open door. There, she found a bluebottle – the same one as before, who knows – caught in a spider's web, legs compromised but wings vibrating freely. A small red-brown spider, much smaller than the fly, crouched at the edge of the scene, near the small gap between the window frame and the wall that was her lair, then moved fluently across to the fly, as if she had been waiting for

T to bear witness.

The fly's desperate efforts made the web bounce. The spider paused again, and when the fly stopped moving, dashed in and spun a fine silvery thread over the fly's proboscis and eyes, going round and round with the speed and dexterity of nothing T had ever seen. She stood transfixed, not sure whether to intervene, or what intervention might look like or achieve. It was too late for the fly, she knew that, and as it – she did not think *he* or *she* – grew weaker, the spider retreated and returned, tightening the bindings.

Still, she worried that she should at least try to save the fly, that not doing so said something about her, to God, to herself, or anyone else who might be watching. Several minutes passed in this hovering way, and as the spider finally dragged her meal, suffocating but not yet dead, towards the gap in the wall, T noticed for the first time how beautiful the fly was, its delicate wings like blown glass, the intricate mechanics connecting these to the iridescent armour of its blue-green back, the topaz domes of its eyes.

Satin, she thought, as she went back to her screen; it would have to be satin.

¶ *I enjoy my walks now that the summer has come. Often I feel I could go far longer than Father has prescribed, but I never do as there would be hell to pay. The other day he surprised me with a visit after lunch and found I was not resting as I should have been – I was only writing to Frances, but he was angrier than I have seen him in some time and said that if I don't get better it will be on my own head, not his. He tells me I'm weak but for some time now I've felt stronger. When I tell him so, he shakes his head and says his ears don't lie, meaning he can hear in my chest that all is not well, it's just as it was. Or worse? He neither confirms nor denies, but his face is like thunder. He says I should count myself lucky he is not overloading me with lard and cheese banquets thrice a day all washed down with pints of hot milk, which he says they still prescribe on the Continent. I eat just the same as everyone else, as if I were still at home, except I'm sure Margaret has increased the portion sizes as I'm struggling to finish, and sometimes she surprises me with 'extras' – the first gooseberry tart of the season this evening – a thrill! – drowning in cream, with spade loads of sugar to make up for the underripe fruit. Bessie still carts everything over with Charlie, when he is home, silverware and all, which she sets out on my little table by the bed, with a white cloth. Mustn't let standards slip, says Mother, though I would have thought they might have by now. Has it been years or only months? The clock is wound differently here. Sometimes while I eat, I try to measure time by my own chewing; sometimes I try to make the movements of my jaw coincide with the beating of my heart. But it happens that I can't hear it and then I panic. I long for someone to share my mealtimes, to distract me from myself and my topsy-turvy reflection in the spoon. Charlie says he'll bring the toasting fork one evening soon and we can make a fire and brown teacakes after sunset, like a couple of frontiersmen after a hard day's panning. I look forward to that. The nights are warm but still so dark.*

VIII.

Sometimes she thought she must be further from Annie than when she had started, and the whole thing was futile, absurd. To make a woman out of so little. She was spending more time reading about other things because she had so quickly exhausted the vanishingly small amount she could unearth about Annie. When she did find something, something that might connect to her in even the most tangential way, she got hooked, only realizing when she came up for air hours or days later that she had lost sight of land. It was like a police investigation, she told herself, and she was the detective: she had a duty to follow all lines of enquiry, whether they pointed towards or away from the matter immediately at hand. She didn't say 'crime' because there was no body, yet.

In fact, everything about Annie was missing: the records, apart from two conflicting birth certificates, were nowhere to be found. No death certificate came up in her searches – the local historians confirmed the same – and although this didn't really surprise T given the uncertainty about Annie's name and date of birth, it didn't satisfy either. She tried 'Ann', 'Annie', 'Anne', 'Elizabeth Anne', 'Elizabeth Annie', and various combinations, but either it turned up thousands of potential matches, none of them right, or there was nothing there at all. '0 results found. Broaden your search for more results.' So she would move on and tell herself that if she just kept reading around Annie, fingering the edges of the puzzle, eventually something would come along to plug the gaps and – she didn't know how the sentence ended.

One evening, after A had been bathed and put to bed, T was on the sofa searching for information about a place she had known as a child, an old villa where her parents' friends had lived many years ago. After the eighteenth-century family who originally owned it died, the vast baroque residence had been divided and sold off as flats and the elaborate and extensive grounds became a shared garden, complete with a labyrinth and sweeping staircases leading to fountains and lilied ponds. She was looking for pictures that would corroborate her memories.

She had seen her sister earlier that day and told her about Annie, updating her on what she had found out so far: the contradictory birth certificates, the tuberculosis, the folly that wasn't any old folly, the mysteriously unregistered death. She had told her that she wanted to go up there to see if she could find out more in person, with the urgency of someone trying to solve a recent disappearance rather than one more than a century old. Her sister hadn't seemed to be listening. T had brought A, so both adults were trying to keep the child's waving hands and legs clear of their coffees, and their conversation kept being sidelined by her emphatic chatter. She had just learnt to say 'more', and when they asked her 'more of what?' she wafted her hands around as if to say, 'Oh, everything.'

At some point, T's sister had reminded her about the villa, that there had been a folly there, too: an elaborate turreted nymphaeum, which they used to dance across, while back up at the house the adults talked about work and politics.

'They said Verdi came to stay and put on a performance of *La Traviata*.'

The instant her sister had said it she'd remembered it herself – the two things almost simultaneous, like the flick of a switch and the light coming on, so that you almost couldn't say which came first, the spark of the story or the memory of it. She saw it through her child-eyes, her sister and her racing across scrunching gravel, piercing the stately grounds with operatic warbles that gave way to hysterical laughter. They had no idea of the opera's tragic themes, that they were prancing and giggling and mock-swooning about a tuberculous woman dying alone.

That evening, while she looked at photographs of the old estate on her laptop, every bit as magical as she recalled, the television was on, its volume turned down to a low murmur. That drama about the women and the nuns again. Colourful shapes quivered at the edges of sight like the spinning lantern she had had at her bedside as a child, whose carnival scenes splashed across the walls whenever the lights went out. Her husband was downstairs in the kitchen making dinner while on the phone to his sister, who must have asked him what T was working on. She had recently quit her job as an editor and the whole family was wondering what she was going to do with her life.

She's writing about a woman, he said. About a woman who...

...

You remember when dad and I went on that walk a while back, the long one?

...

Yeah, well, there was a folly that a woman lived in, sometime in the 1800s, I think...

...

You know, a building with no real purpose, for show...

...

Yeah, and so I read about it on a plaque and then I told her and, I don't know, it sort of... caught her, I guess... her imagination, I mean...

...

Yeah.

And the conversation moved on.

'Consumed,' T said to herself; the word he was looking for was consumed.

The next day, she booked a train ticket.

·

T was in touch with an archivist, who had agreed to meet her at the tower – she wouldn't be able to get in otherwise, the archivist had said, because it was private property and only she held the key. The tower belonged to a prestigious fee-paying school that had owned the entire estate since the mid-1930s, when the family sold it off for £2,700, around £235,000 in today's money. It didn't seem much for such opulent real estate.

The archivist had sent a brief history of the tower, a draft document composed in the run up to its renovation some years before. It began: 'The original purpose of [REDACTION] is unclear.'

(The redaction is mine. The locals have a nickname for the tower, derived from its faint resemblance to an old-fashioned cruet, but it does not help our story to know this.)

'[REDACTION] is thought to have been built as an isolation house for Charles's daughter,' the document continued;

Anne developed Tuberculosis at the age of 18 and rather than send his daughter away to live in a sanatorium he built [REDACTION]. This allowed Anne to live close to her family without contaminating them.... Anne is thought to have survived for just three years before dying at the age of 21.

An alternative theory was also offered: that the tower might have been built as a dining suite, a popular architectural feature among wealthy estate owners at the turn of the century, offering an outdoors-indoors experience, an artful framing of nature. But T noticed that the theory, set out in a letter to the school by someone employed in the 'Interpretation Office' of the local authorities – the archivist had sent T a copy – did not appear in the final, published history, nor anywhere else on the school's website which dedicated several pages to the tower. Clearly the notion had been discredited.

The history cited Charles's death in 1924 as a decisive moment in the story of the house. The family, which T presumed meant Charles Jnr and his mother Alice, put the house up for sale along with its entire contents. They apparently wanted none of it and left as soon as they could. But while the contents sold well – there must have been much to admire among the family's possessions – the house remained vacant for more than a decade, until sale to the school was agreed and a final auction stripped the place to its barest bones. Then, less than twenty years after Charles had it built, the house was demolished.

The archivist had sent scans of the original sale brochure from 1938, announcing the auction in a cacophony of capital letters of varying size and girth, of 'the whole of the valuable interior & exterior fixtures & fittings in and about the property previous to the demolition of the mansion.' Everything must go: 60 oak- and pine-panelled doors, 60 sash and casement windows, 1,400 square feet of oak and mahogany panelling, a 'HANDSOME OAK STAIRCASE with Double Handrail and Tapered Balustrades, 20 Mantelpieces and Grates, Dresser and China Cupboard Fitments, Lavatory and Bathroom Fittings, Radiators, Cooking Ranges, Copper Cylinder'.

And more and more, right down to a 'PAIR OF HANDSOME WROUGHT IRON GATES with 2 side gates and 4 Stone-Built Pillars', and a 'Stone built two-storied SUMMER HOUSE, providing a fine view point' – as if the view could be taken away with it.

It was the shopping list Charles had compiled with his architect in 1905, except now the directions of travel, material and monetary, were reversed, and the building disappeared detail by detail, like peaks of bubble bath in a drained tub. How sad, T thought, that the family home should be dissolved in this way, Charles's pride dismembered and sold in lots to the highest bidder. Perhaps vanity had made him overstretch and his death revealed finances in disarray; the surviving family had no choice but to leave. Or perhaps, T thought, the place reminded them too much of Annie, so that whenever anyone else played her piano they imagined they could hear her voice, sometimes fluent sometimes brittle, singing in the oak-panelled walls.

She tried to see the brochure as an opportunity to rebuild, to give the family the setting she had so far struggled to conjure up, not having the imagination of a novelist. Now, she had facts: that most of the twenty mantelpieces were a mixture of black and white marble, for instance; that the taps in the bathrooms were plated (likely gold), the toilets encased in mahogany, and the white enamel baths 'fitted for shower and spray', which, she thought, would not have been mentioned were the technology not remarkable and covetable. She knew now about the L-shaped aviary adjoined to the spacious conservatory, both with glossy black-and-white chessboard tiles. And she knew that the master bedroom had a large, double-door iron fireproof wall safe. No one will ever know what it contained.

As she worked her way through, item by item, she had the impression of a small-scale coming together, as if she were building a doll's house, complete with electricity, wrought iron weathervane, copper-covered cupola and lightning conductor. It seemed a condition of the reconstitution that the house be miniaturized, so that her mind could take it all in from above. So she didn't get lost in it. And she began to see quite clearly now the mahogany-panelled drawing room with its white marble mantelpiece of plain panel pilasters and a carved centre panel of fruit and flowers (she confirmed her interpretation of the words against a slew of period-specific images online). And she could see Charles standing there, one elbow on the mantel for support, as he explained to the family that they were lucky to have caught it early, that most people, not having his training and experience, would not have suspected it at all; and how lucky, truly lucky, that they would be able to keep Annie close, that with just a few minor adjustments their summer house could be converted into a sanatorium, quite state of the art, why not, entirely under his care, of course, so that no one need suffer her being sent away.

(She had not baked this man from scratch – I should say – but rather had poured the essence of another man into an otherwise insubstantial batter. Early on, Charles had blended in her mind with Leslie Stephen, as described with undimmed feeling thirty-five years after his death, by his daughter Virginia Woolf, another middle child: he is 'the exacting, the violent, the histrionic, the demonstrative, the self-centred, the self-pitying, the deaf, the appealing, the alternately loved and hated father'. Try as she might, she couldn't unmix them now.)

T imagined the women of the family sitting at the edges of Charles's makeshift stage, on sofas and chaises of yellow-gold satin. She had Alice smoothing her skirts to avoid looking at her children until she was sure of her own composure (to show fear would have been to signal doubt in her husband). Beside Alice she set Emmeline, with eyes darting back and forth between her father and younger sister, as if lines in the air between them told the story of what came next. Charles Jnr broke the silence with a raised glass, the dregs of dinner's claret, and said, 'Hear hear, to Father, to Annie and us all, our good health!'

And Annie, what did she feel? T pictured her, watery eyed and waxen as her thoughts turned to the tower. But as much as she tried to animate the scene, she knew it didn't work. She herself was unconvinced by what she saw. The materials were thin; she had pressed too hard or used the wrong glue. Everything went to pieces again.

Instead, she wondered where the brochure's 303 lots ended up, how far they travelled and to what use they were put; how many hands, and whose, have turned the family's gold-plated taps, how many naked backs reclined against the cool enamel of the roll-top bath. Which winds move their weathervane now, and how many times has lightning struck?

T once lived around the corner from a reclamation yard laid out between railway arches and remembered how at weekends, she and her not-yet husband spent hours wandering around with take-out coffees, marvelling at sumptuous stone fireplaces, Victorian science-lab tables, rows of old theatre seats in crimson velvet, a gargantuan Grecian pillar lying bashfully on her side in the dirt. Everything was too big – 'look at the *size* of this!', she'd say, pointing at a rosewood dining table for thirty-six or so guests, imagining trying to squeeze it into their one-bed second-floor apartment. Even small or ordinary things – a modest side-table, guilt-brass table lamps, rusty garden tools – seemed somehow outsized, as if by a trick of perspective. Something about their pastness, the invisible quantity of history, made them swell so that the very idea of owning them in the present – of resting a can of beer on them, say, or a television – seemed to her ludicrous.

It's funny, she thought, how we can think of something as ours no matter who made it, and how many people have owned it before us, just because we're the most recent to have claimed it. She understood the fundamentals of buying and selling, but there was, she felt, an underlying psychic continuity – those were her words – that property laws couldn't touch. She remembered Carl Jung's description of the soul as an 'endlessly varied recombination of age-old components', 'forever coming into being and passing on', and thought that he might equally have been describing a home filled with objects from that reclamation yard and others like it. 'It is as if a silent, greater family, stretching down the centuries, were peopling the house,' he said. Whenever you raise that slightly clouded cut-crystal tumbler to your lips, she thought, or flick the delicate switch of a green bankers' lamp, you touch your present to another's, long since passed; you mirror their movements and so, in a way, revive them.

Jung too had had a tower, that was why he was on her mind that day, and his, like Annie's, had been a two-story house, albeit circular rather than octagonal. On the bank of a river feeding Lake Zurich, it was for him alone. As time went by, he said, he had found that something essential was missing in his life, that while his scientific practice had 'put my fantasies and the contents of the unconscious on a solid footing', still 'words and paper... did not seem real enough'. What he needed, he determined, was 'a confession of faith in stone', the ultimate expression and

experience of his psychological beliefs: a tower of, and for, his innermost thoughts. And so, he built it, referring to it ever after with a capital T.

Years later he discovered that the Tower stood on the site of an eighteenth-century mass grave of French soldiers, who had drowned in the river in their dozens under Austrian assault. T imagined Jung erecting its walls, humming something by Bach, whose music he considered the purest expression of the unconscious, oblivious to the world of pain beneath his feet.

She wasn't sure why the detail affected her so, except that something in her always seemed to catch on those moments of discordance, on how a surface smooth and benign could conceal depths of unknown chaos. How the past, present and future could exist in utter ignorance of each other; how reality didn't crack and splinter under the pressure and the worlds didn't seep into each other. And it was one thing, she thought, when the tragedy was far removed from your own serene carry-on, as it was in Jung's case. Quite another when it wasn't; when the past, present and future all played out on the same body, and the future self simply couldn't break through to warn the past self of the coming threat.

Was there no give in time? Had it always to be so rigidly, unfeelingly linear? She thought about how minutes before a bomb dropped someone might be sitting on a park bench, smiling to themselves at the blessing of such fine weather, and the before and after couldn't change each other even slightly. Someone could be so content, she thought, so untouched by pain right up until pain landed in their lap, blowing off their legs. They would never be the same person again and they hadn't seen it coming. But usually someone just a few steps ahead had.

¶ *I have been awake most of the night waiting for a dawn which comes later and later. It's rough, extraordinarily so, not to be able to sleep anymore, but when the darkness falls my mind seems to spark a fire and every thought inside me leans in close, rubbing its hands and turning itself this way and that. By the early hours of the morning the fire is roaring, its flames licking at the back of my eyes, and those ghoulish thoughts are dancing a merry dance. But what dead silence all around. I can hear the squeal of a mouse as it is caught, the triumphant shriek of the owl, and the wind, when it gets up, imitates the wolf to scare us all. They say that whenever an owl cries, a woman somewhere dies – but why do they say it? Why say such things? It is five now and although the sky is black velvet, I will draw a line under yesterday and begin the work of today.*

IX.

Every confident day was followed by a crisis of conviction in the night. Or, if she had had a bad day, when all her
searching and probing led nowhere, she could be almost
certain that in the small hours the weight would shift
like ballast water on a ship; things would feel steadier by
morning.

That night, the night after she had decided to make
the trip, was a bad one. She knew this was because she
had spent money on a train and accommodation and neither was cheap, especially when there were A's nursery
fees to think of, not to mention gas and electricity bills,
which seemed increasingly untethered from the reality
of life in her small house. The money changed things
because money spent on Annie was money that could, or
should, be spent elsewhere, on things less far-fetched,
self-indulgent, insignificant, senseless, mad. Those words
and more came to mind. Money also created an expecta-
tion, she realized: that she would get something substantial
in return. If she didn't, the logic of capitalism dictated,
she would have to consider herself scammed, a gullible
fool. Which in turn implied a third party, a Dr Williams,
except she knew it was her in all directions. Unable
to sleep she slipped out of bed and tiptoed downstairs.

In the kitchen, the wolf looked at her without raising
his head and sighed. He was used to her, knew she was
going nowhere but the laptop. The blue-white light of the
screen was like cold water to her face. The day's work hit
her as if no time had passed since the afternoon, when she
had slammed the screen shut in such a hurry to collect
A. She had been studying Henry Peach Robinson's picture, *Fading Away*, from 1858, wondering how his scene
of tuberculous death compared to Annie's end; whether

Annie's mother and father had been present, too, and her sister – it would have had to be Emmeline – at her head adjusting the pillows, like the nurse in the surgical film. Had Annie died in the tower or, seeing that all was lost, had they brought her home in the nick of time?

In near darkness now, with the gentle swash of the dishwasher running a night-cycle, it was Robinson's process that interested her. She read about how he had sliced up the negatives from four separately photographed subjects, overlaying them with a fifth photograph of the room to make one composite scene in which each figure played its part. The careful, ministering sister and the prim mother sitting at a remove, with her frilly bonnet on as if she had just got back from town; behind them, the father, a jet-black presence like a black hole in the centre of the scene, his back turned, standing against the light of the day, leaning into the window frame, one hand to his brow. She imagined him pinching the bridge of his nose in a studied gesture of focus and emotional continence. The window was open, as you would expect, although storm clouds were gathering; the flowers on a small table beside him had drooped in the chill and dropped a few berries. She remembered Rolleston's magical mistletoe.

And then there was the dying girl, of course, the silver-white foil to her father's blackness. T guessed she was about fifteen, her bloodless lips slightly parted, her eyes all but closed, in a head that appeared only vaguely connected to the knot of bedsheets and blankets beneath it. She noticed a book discarded on the seat beside the girl, presumably by her sister, who had been reading aloud until things took a turn for the worst. An accompanying inscription – 'must then that peerless form... that lovely outline which is fair as breathing marble, perish?' – was from Percy Shelley's *Queen Mab*, a fairy tale

83

about a brighter, more compassionate future. Robinson, a painter turned photographer, was criticized for this morbid scene, T read, for making public such intimate pain, in a society contingent on secret suffering. As well as impropriety he was accused of artificiality, of subverting the purpose of photography. A photograph should document reality, detractors said, not create another. T wondered what had angered people most: that they had been brought face to face with a private tragedy, or that it was all make-believe and they had been tricked, like simpletons, into real feelings. That the images had brought money and fame, enough to transform Robinson's ailing photography studio, was another bone of contention.

Robinson was a pictorialist, arguably the first, and valued artistic expression above realism. The difference between taking and making a photograph was everything. 'A work of art is a work of order,' he said, thirty years after the furore over *Fading Away* had died down, 'and if the artist is to put the stamp of his own mind on his work, he must arrange, modify, and dispose of his materials so that they may appear in a more agreeable and beautiful manner than they would have assumed without his interference.' The word 'interference' didn't sound to T neutral; she wondered if it ever had. ('Agreeable' and 'beautiful' she wrote down on a scrap of paper.) She remembered a line from Bashkirtseff's journal: 'There is nothing in the world to compare with Art; one regards those outlines, those shadings, with respect, with emotion – one is creator, one feels oneself almost great.' It had seemed an odd thing to say, for a self-professed naturalist bent on conveying the 'exact, the absolute, the strict truth' without false lighting and other tricks of distortion. Robinson would have dropped the 'almost'.

She cast an eye over a series of bucolic scenes in which

FADING AWAY.

Photographed from nature by Henry P. Robinson, Leamington.

children cavorted among trees and pretty maidens prepared flowers for market, and read that Robinson used costumed actors or well-known members of society as models; real countryfolk lacked the qualities he sought to convey. His intension was to re-enchant his audience with a world that conventional photography flatly replicated until they grew tired of it. 'The photograph told us everything about the facts of nature and left out the mystery,' he said. 'Now, however hard-headed a man may be, he cannot stand too many facts; it is easy to get a surfeit of realities, and he wants a little mystification as a relief.' Here, she thought, was art giddily gifting reality a dose of what it needed.

Perhaps inevitably, that same impulse drew Robinson to fairy tales. In the same year as *Fading Away* he created a four-image series retelling the story of Little Red Riding Hood, the penultimate, and in T's view best, of which captured the moment the sweet heroine realized things were not what they seemed: a grotesque wolf's head (taxidermized) peeps out from between the covers where her mother had said her sick grandmother would be; Little Red recoils in a stilted demi-plié, dropping her basket of bread. A final picture shows Little Red back where she started, in her mother's kitchen, safe and grateful, the lesson learnt. (But what was it again? About always listening to your mother? Not trusting strangers? Never taking a shortcut unless you're looking for trouble?)

Though Robinson didn't show the *how* of the in-between, T knew what Little Red, trapped in the horror of her present, could not: that a brave huntsman had been nearby the whole time and, as soon as the little girl was eaten – which the wolf's prominent fangs suggested was likely – he would rush in and cut her out of the beast's belly with a sharp blade, restoring order and bringing the gift of happy-ever-after. How amazing, the critics said, that Robinson was around 'once upon a time' to capture events unfolding!

But while they were fretting about fact and fiction and the increasingly murky space between the two, Robinson's photographs had achieved something far more consequential: by a classic example of the distraction technique beloved of magicians and pickpockets, Robinson had relieved the photographed subject of her powers of self-possession. These were now under the control of someone else, beyond the picture's edge. Little Red could be anything Robinson wanted her to be now, anywhere and at any time, with or without her knowledge.

The ragged breath of T's own wolf returned her to the kitchen at 4.20 a.m. He was dreaming, his whole body absorbed in that interior world, leg muscles flexing, claws tensing and untensing; three shadow barks broke the silence. As she clicked the laptop shut, the wolf lifted his head and she wondered if he was relieved to be back there with her, rather than giving chase or being chased in the woods of his imagination. Did he even know he had been somewhere else?

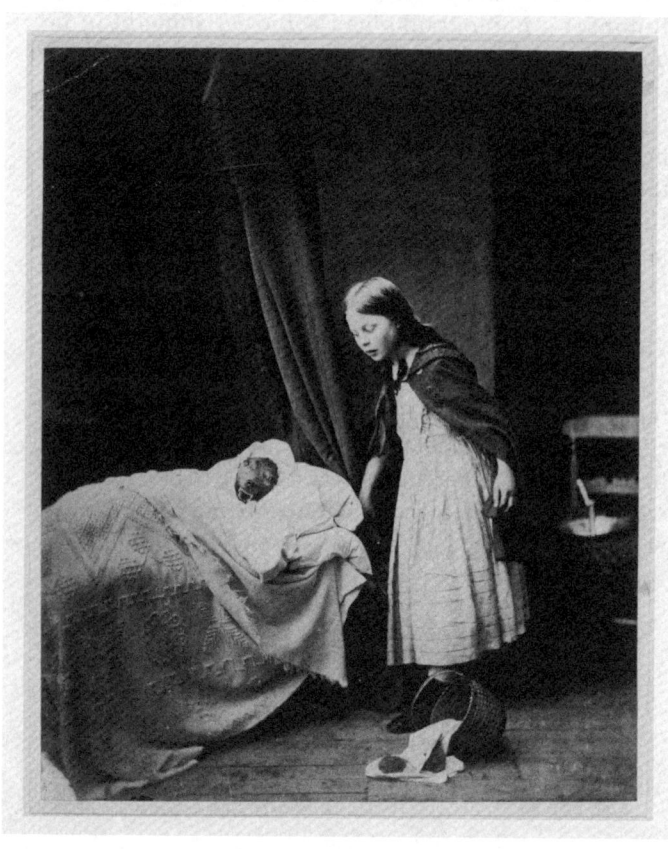

¶ It's already light. I've been awake for hours listening to the birds recount their dreams and nightmares, waiting for the pain between my shoulder blades to pass. Aches that seem to split my back in two. There's stiffness in every limb. For hours I seem to lie there, my body set in marble. A new development. And all the while my chest creaks and burns like a bonfire, so hot that I seem to feel it through my clothes. But I do drift off somehow, and must dream, for I see wild apparitions, dancing shadows at the edge of my vision, and hear them too, singing in a kind of chorus that rises and falls like the sea. I'm frightened and can do nothing but blink and observe the room around me, looking exactly as when I last saw it, exactly as it does in real life. As if I weren't dreaming at all. Who can explain it? All I want when one of these fits comes over me is to fly through the open window and dive into the icy river, to float on my back and let it take me, to stare wide-eyed into the sky so the light goes deeper and deeper, as deep as it needs to go.

X.

She set off early one morning from the far south of the country, with hundreds of miles to go before she would come within touching distance of the northern edge. Not that it would take long; five or six hours and she would be there, on tracks that a century before had so well served Dr Williams, distributing both the newspapers that advertised his miracle cure and hundreds of thousands of the pills themselves. It seemed funny to her that the same network that had facilitated the spread of those fantastical stories of recovery, of transformations so magical Lewis Carroll himself might have written them, had in other ways reduced people's stock in wonderment. As ever faster trains diminished remoteness, the cloak of strangeness that used to accompany the traveller and his tales of faraway people and places fell soundlessly away.

She had read a review a few days earlier of *The Book of Wonderful Characters,* a re-edition of a late nineteenth-century compendium with a helpfully thorough subtitle: 'Memoirs and Anecdotes of Remarkable and Eccentric Persons in All Ages and Countries'. Among the stories told were those of a man who lived to the age of 152, having been painted by Rubens in his 140th year; of Dirty Dick, who stopped washing after his beloved died suddenly on their wedding day; and of a woman who survived on the smell of flowers alone. A preface written in 1869 complained that, 'We have nearly lost all, and are daily losing what little remains of, our individuality'; 'all people and all places seem now to be alike; and the railways are, no doubt, the principal cause of this change.' If we all end up alike, the writer asks, about a century before the word 'globalization' entered most people's lexicon, what stories could we possibly have to tell each other?

It had reminded T of an essay by Walter Benjamin, published in 1936, in which he said that the art of storytelling was coming to an end. Only three years before he wrote the essay, a Boeing plane had carried passengers from one side of America to the other in fewer than twenty hours, and yet, she thought, Benjamin seemed less concerned with modern travel snuffing out fantastical stories by making everyone alike, less worthy of a tale, than with a dearth of storytellers. 'Less and less frequently do we encounter people with the ability to tell a tale properly,' he said. 'It is as if something that seemed inalienable to us, the securest among our possessions, were taken from us: the ability to exchange experiences.'

For Benjamin, she knew, this had to do with the rise of mass media and its privileging of new, promptly verifiable information over the older kind of story, the kind we have been telling since the first fires were lit if not before; stories in which the teller, in exchange for entertainment, a moment's transport, asks for nothing short of the listener's faith. 'The intelligence that came from afar,' he said, 'whether the spatial kind from foreign countries or the temporal kind of tradition – possessed an authority which gave it validity, even when it was not subject to verification.' But the emphasis now, Benjamin said, was on explanation and plausibility; and miracles – I needn't tell you – are nothing if not inexplicable and implausible. Information was 'incompatible with the spirit of storytelling', he said. 'It is half of the art of storytelling to keep a story free from explanation.'

T must have intuited this, because the truth was that she could have travelled up to see Annie's tower for herself all along, could have made more incisive enquiries of the historians, could have discovered what actually occurred and possibly explained the whole thing away.

More information could no doubt have been isolated in the many archives; she could certainly have been more rigorous. The truth, which I'm not sure she had started to suspect quite yet – we're getting ahead of ourselves – was that she hadn't wanted to find out more, hadn't wanted to add shade to Annie's portrait and fill in the space she had come to represent: a space of mystery and possibility, a reservoir of unverifiable and almost, but not absolutely, unbelievable happening. She hadn't wanted to know, once and for all, what had become of Annie, to know if there was a body and, if so, where it was and how it got there. Hadn't wanted to consider the matter settled, the story told and a life reduced to its happenings, as if the rest – the endless possibility that surrounds every person like fog – had never existed.

But she didn't know this yet, and, so, with the inevitability of falling dominoes, she was on a train, travelling backwards, heading north, to the start; to the source.

.

From early morning the sky had been overcast with clouds. The land on both sides of the train was below water the colour of lead. It had been raining for weeks. Every inch of sky was as if padded with dirty wool; there were more storms to come. The lights inside the train were harsh, neon, so that everything was reflected in the windows, cast against the rolling dark. As the train cut up the country, the severed torsos of passengers drifted alongside.

Everyone was staring at miniature screens, held in the palms of their hands like pocket mirrors. On the radio a few days earlier, she had heard a woman speak nostalgically of a time before phones had taken away idle hours, when we might have spoken to strangers, asking questions about where they had come from and where they were going. Now, we send messages to people who aren't there and find other ways to fill the silence. It's as if we can't bear to just sit with time, the woman had said; as if, fearing its unknown possibilities, we must distract ourselves from it. 'Put the phone down,' she pleaded, 'dream, and think about who you really are.' (On the other side of the aisle from T, a mother whispered to her young son, 'Put the screen down love, look out of the window, rest your eyes'; dream.)

The woman next to T was watching a programme about extravagantly wealthy women, who lived in vast stuccoed palaces in distant pink hills, high above the rest of us. The super-saturated colours and blunt cuts caught T's eye like strobing lights; the word REAL flashed across the screen at regular intervals. They unhinged her, those programmes, the way they blurred fact and fiction and made a mockery of both, how they played fast and loose with time, reordering people's lives to fit a narrative arc devised in the writers' room. Something about the spirit was off, she thought, less distasteful than recklessly, cruelly disorientating; how you were asked to believe and not believe at the same time.

Turning to the window on her right and feeling its cold against her shoulder, her belongings on the table bounced back at her in the glass, framed like a still life: a laptop, a bottle of water, a banana and a KitKat, a pile of three books. A woman with Joan of Arc hair peered up at her with fierce eyes – black, all pupil – from the cover of the top book: Katherine Mansfield, in a scarlet square-necked jersey, her cheeks daubed with grey, green, peach and a touch of the same scarlet. The smear on her left cheek, like fresh blood, the artist's parting touch. Tuberculosis had been with Mansfield for about two years by then.

T had been spending time with Mansfield, in that battered edition of her letters and journals compiled by the critic and writer C. K. Stead, sometime in the 1970s. Bought second-hand on the strength of its cover, the suffocating red-on-red oils painted by Mansfield's friend Anne Rice, the book had been forgotten entirely – T had not seen it in more than a decade, in fact – until a few weeks before her trip, when she had followed a series of stepping stones, reading one thing which led to another and then another, which led to Mansfield. When she pulled the book out and started reading, the moment felt contrived, as if the *she* of all those years ago had set things up for the *she* of today.

The book's spine was so used that Mansfield's name was consumed by the creases. To read her, T found, was to almost feel the advance of tuberculosis eating away at the body and mind until nothing was left. She read of the searing sensation Mansfield called 'the flat-iron', the 'appalling burn', the 'deafening creak' in her left lung, insomnia and night terrors, 'and, oh God, this terrifying idea that one must die, and may be going to die'. The sweet, fleeting relief found in lifting one arm over the head, like a forlorn ballerina.

She was quick to notice biographical coincidences between Mansfield and Annie, albeit – she would have conceded it herself – the sort you might only spot in the right light: that Mansfield, born in 1888, was an almost exact contemporary of Annie's, and the middle one of five children in a fabulously wealthy family. Like Annie, the name on her birth certificate, Kathleen, diverged from the name she was known by. Mansfield's mother was called Annie, in fact. These details will not seem much to you or me, but to T, then, they felt like what she had been missing; something to cling to, to climb.

According to the biographer Claire Tomalin, T read, Mansfield's middle-sibling status cast the die of her world view. She was, in her own words, 'the odd man out of the family – the ugly duckling', a 'thundercloud' in the family's clear, cold sky. 'But to be the odd one, the difficult one, not understood, separate,' Tomalin pointed out, 'is also a privileged position, the position of Cinderella.' In the fairy tales she was raised on, Mansfield discovered an outlet for darker feelings that lay latent in this 'nice', bourgeois family. If there were beautiful slumbering princesses there were also dastardly crones masquerading as kindly old ladies; if there was true love, there were also jealousy, hatred, apparently random acts of cruelty. (I say 'apparently' because the adult knows there is always some logic.) Her stories are full of supposedly trustworthy adults with hidden agendas, of people who say one thing and mean, or do, another. A gentleman admirer with wolfish teeth; a neighbour 'so incredibly handsome that he looked like a mask or a most perfect illustration in an American novel', who reveals himself to be a predator; a father 'so big... especially his mouth when he yawned' that to think of him was 'like thinking about a giant'. So ingrained was Mansfield's cosmology that it absorbed the tuberculosis with which she was diagnosed at twenty-eight, drawing it into that otherworldly realm, whose language was portentous animals, monsters, bodily transformations, unlikely twists, and the stark and eternal confrontation between good and evil.

At first, before the severity of the condition was known, T encountered Mansfield as a fly. 'I'll tell you exactly what I feel like,' she wrote to her husband John Middleton Murry, from Bandol in the South of France, where she was in exile from more noxious climes. 'I feel like a fly who has been dropped into the milk-jug and fished out again, but is still too milky and drowned to start cleaning up yet.' (How like Mansfield to infect something as wholesome as milk.) Next, the disease 'is like a big wild dog who followed me home one day and has taken a most unpleasant fancy to me'. Elsewhere, 'a very dark, obscure, frightening thing seems to rise up in my soul', and a 'loathsome ... toad' squats on her chest; and all the while 'there is a great black bird flying over me.... I don't know exactly what *kind* he is'. T imagined each creature in turn and recalled the nursery rhyme about the old lady who swallowed a fly. Its jolly refrain: 'Perhaps she'll die!'

From the depths of her loneliness Mansfield wrote to Murry, who seemed reluctant to leave London to join her:

> I feel so awfully like a tiny girl whom someone has locked up in the dark cupboard, even though it's daytime. I don't want to bang at the door or make a noise, but I want you to come with a key you've made yourself and let me out, and then we should tiptoe away together into a kinder place where everybody was more of our heart and size.

As T read Mansfield's words, she was moved less by the childish imagery than by the realization that Annie possibly, probably, never knew what it was to pine for someone. Someone real, she meant, a figure more substantial than the princely characters that paraded from the pages of her books. She was eighteen when she entered the tower and couldn't have had even a shade of the experience of Mansfield, who lived across continents for thirty-four years, albeit not well. She wondered if it would have made the solitude easier or more difficult for Annie to bear. In 1908, when Annie entered the tower, all but ending her connection with the world, Mansfield was on a ship, from

96

her native New Zealand to London, where she had convinced her parents she must live if she was to make it as an artist. And, 'in the joyous mood of the successful rebel', Tomalin said, she was headed straight for her 'first foray into sexual freedom'.

One of Mansfield's early lovers introduced her to the stories of Chekhov, who would influence her more than any other writer. Chekhov had died of tuberculosis in 1904, a detail that to a healthy twenty-year-old might have seemed tragic and romantic in a remote kind of way. But in a turn of events that 'in a work of fiction', Tomalin said, 'would appear so extraordinary and melodramatic that one might shrug it off as improbable', the same lover also gave Mansfield gonorrhoea. In 1910, a bungled operation removed one of her fallopian tubes and introduced the infection to the bloodstream, the painful consequences of which plagued Mansfield until the end, becoming enmeshed with the symptoms of the tuberculosis she caught about six years later. Gonorrhoea had probably made her more susceptible.

From then, T read, misfortune struck Mansfield with the leaden predictability of tolling bells. No one could blame her for feeling persecuted by reality, for wanting to duck and dive her way through it. At times in the journal Mansfield refers to herself in the third person – 'it's simply incredible, watching K.M., to see how little causes a panic. She's a perfect corker at toppling over'– as if she had become separated from herself and was now watching her own life, documenting it with a wry detachment. The pressure of reality had cracked the mirror and made her many and other. In her thirty-odd years she was also, and not exclusively: Kass, Katie, Katya, Julian Mark, Katherine Schönfeld, Matilda Berry, Kathleen Bowden, Katharina, Katiushka, Kissienka, Kezia, Rewa, Tui,

Elizabeth Stanley, Tig or Tiger and Mrs K. Bendall. Once or twice, she was Ariadne, the Greek princess abandoned on a rocky island by the man she trusted and loved.

Mansfield's editor recalled that the writer's 'great delight was a game she played of being someone else', when she would claim the part 'completely until she even got herself mixed up as to who and what she was'. Tomalin, T found, was blunter, less tolerant of the impulse to deceive, more wary of the less innocent implications of the game: 'Katherine was a liar all her life,' she said, 'a bold and elaborate inventor of false versions.... If the truth was dull, it could be artistically embroidered; and if she was the heroine of her own life story, lies became not lies but fiction, a perfectly respectable thing.'

Hope took many guises, too, and yet, T noticed, it was always male. Although Mansfield determinedly, and against medical advice, refused to enter a sanatorium, this did not prevent her seeking out doctor after doctor, each professing himself able to vanquish the disease in ever more wonderous ways. The fact was these men, cherry-picking from among their patients, probably believed it themselves. Mansfield, though, whose early life had awakened her to the idea that a hero could also be a villain, towards the end had come to expect it. Of Ivan Manoukhin, a Russian émigré practising in Paris, who claimed in 1922 to be able to cure her by flooding the spleen with X-rays, she wrote: 'I have the feeling that M. is a really good man. I have also a sneaking feeling (I use that word "sneaking" advisedly) that he is a kind of unscrupulous impostor.'

Where exactly are the frontiers between lies and fiction and the creations of belief, T wondered, between the con artist, the storyteller and the priest? Does it matter if the person drawn in dies with hope in their heart?

Yes and no. Yes. But also no.

When the doctors inevitably let her down, Mansfield fell back wholeheartedly into the thick softness of older, more established fantasies. To Murry stealing through the locked door with a charmed key; to her father, Harold Beauchamp, arriving from abroad to sweep her off her feet and remind her of the wonderous world in which she had grown up. 'To be held and kissed and called my precious child was almost too much,' she wrote to Murry. Each attachment was its own kind of drug.

Reading Tomalin's account of Mansfield's ambivalence towards her father, T couldn't help but imagine Annie and Charles onto the page: 'He might be vulgar, crass, tight-fisted, but he was also strong, reliable and magically rich,' and whenever she felt little and lost, he appeared 'glamorous and omnipotent'. And when, writing to Rice, Mansfield described her father as 'a kind of vast symbolic chapeau out of which I shall draw the little piece of paper that will decide my Fate', T thought of the flickering fortune-telling goldfish, with its improvised lies and strange authority. Mansfield trusted her father, she thought; she had faith in him. Had he insisted, would she have gone to a sanatorium? Would it have worked? Probably not, she thought, but it might have given her a few more years to live and work, and something else to believe in.

•

The journal had turned out to be a bit of a lie, really. Had T read Stead's introduction before embarking on the thing, rather than saving it till the end as was her habit, born of a fear of spoilers, she would have known. Instead, she had been deceived. But then deception was so much a part of the Mansfield experience.

She had found an article in which a scholar, Anna Jackson, described the mass of papers left to Murry by Mansfield on her death, including forty-six notebooks, exercise books, engagement diaries, bundles of loose pages and torn pieces of paper. 'Each notebook is in itself,' T read,

> a collection of beginnings of various writing projects. Exercise books that begin being kept as a diary turn into recipe books or notebooks for first drafts of stories or are turned to some other use, while collections of poems, notes on Shakespeare, and other projects, are turned into diaries, or have diary entries randomly placed within them.... In fact it is not quite accurate to call them "entries" since few of them were "entered" into any sort of ongoing text.... The passages were written at different times, in different books....

A world of scraps from which to assemble versions of a woman, never the same twice.

'I should like him to publish as little as possible and tear up and burn as much as possible he will understand that I desire to leave as few traces of my camping ground as possible,' Mansfield wrote in a will, about six months before her death. For a writer of precision, T thought, the absent punctuation and repetition of the word 'possible' pointed to unrest. A letter addressed to Murry, written the previous week with instructions that it be opened only after her death, elaborated on her wishes:

> All my manuscripts I leave entirely to you to do what you like with. Go through them one day, dear love, and destroy all you do not use. Please destroy all letters you do not wish

to keep and all papers. You know my love of tidiness. Have a clean sweep ... and leave all fair – will you?

As far as it is possible to know, T read, Murry destroyed nothing, instead producing a 'scrapbook' and three separate editions of the so-called journal. He transcribed as much as he could of Mansfield's notoriously indecipherable handwriting and selected from the single, unsorted mass of manuscripts only that which contributed to the 'pure' (his word) version of Mansfield he sought to create. 'Create' was right, T thought, because she doubted the Mansfield of the journal bore much resemblance to the Mansfield he knew, just as the Murry Mansfield held in her mind as she wrote to him was not the man sitting at his desk in London, thinking of work, of kippers for lunch, of people and things other than her and when they would next be together. 'There is a sense in which neither sought true understanding of the other,' T read in Tomalin's biography. 'For each of them, the other became a symbolic figure very early on: she the good, suffering, spontaneous genius, he the ideally beautiful scholar-lover without whom neither life nor death could be properly contemplated. Each settled to a dream-version of the other.' They were mutual editors, in real-time, intent on their own narrative arc.

It was fitting, T supposed, for a writer whose stories hinged on judiciously elided details, so that events might concern unnamed characters, unfold in an unnamed country or come to an abrupt non-ending, that so much of her own life should be left out in this way. But it brought another person to the edge of vision. Who was the shady editor? What were his intentions? By what sleight of hand did he accomplish them?

'A work of art is a work of order'; T remembered the

101

line of Henry Peach Robinson's, had known it would return to the surface soon enough. The artist must arrange, modify, and dispose of his materials, and leave things in a manner more agreeable and beautiful than that in which he found them.

Leave all fair – will you?

T pictured the strong smooth back of a goddess slowly revolving, a delicate scar suspended like silk threads between her shoulder blades. The perfectly preserved line of her neck dipping down to her breastbone.

By 'beauty' what was really meant, T thought, was effective, powerful, able to get under the skin – words with more manipulative connotations. Murry's and Stead's compositions were rigorous exercises in telescopic empathy, and she didn't deny that in reading them her emotions had got the better of her, that she had been moved to tears, feeling herself at the end carried to the threshold of Mansfield's room in 1923, to await the doctor's verdict; to know, as though she didn't already, if it really was over this time.

When the extent of Murry's interference (to use Robinson's word) was revealed on his death in 1957, it must have felt, T thought, like discovering that what you thought was the ceiling was in fact the floor of a congested attic. Realizing the full extent and shape of the original manuscripts, the critic Ian Gordon described Murry's journals as 'a brilliant piece of literary synthesis and editorial patchwork'. He confirmed that Murry had invented nothing, but was troubled by the discrepancy between the 'scrappier, less tidy' reality of Mansfield's manuscripts and the neat and satisfying flow of Murry's production. 'It is hardly too much to claim', he said, 'that [the journal] is as much Murry's work as Katherine Mansfield's'.

Although, by the time Stead set about his task, the

original manuscripts had become available, their illegibility made them all but inaccessible, so, for the volume T had with her on the train that day, Stead could only consult Murry's composite portrait, forming his own with the same materials, rearranged if no less 'real'. Only in 2000 were the manuscripts transcribed in their entirety, by Margaret Scott, a woman who appeared to possess the charmed key to the Mansfield scrawl. Thanks to Scott, an unredacted Mansfield appeared for the first (or second) time and with it the story of a messy, 'impure' woman. There, Jackson, the scholar who had first alerted T to the duplicity of the book in her possession, encountered,

> a KM who moves from the poetic mode to the mundane, almost in the same breath. This is a kitchen KM, a laundry KM, a KM who scribbles flights of fancy in amongst her shopping lists, a KM who sits down to write a story but gives up halfway through to think about her wardrobe and plan new additions to it. This is a KM who wills herself to be poetic, who forces herself to write, but lapses easily into distraction: so many unfinished stories, so many plans for novels. The pudding recipes in between plans for great works suggest she left off writing to go and bake.

T wondered which vision of herself Mansfield would have preferred to see out in the world: Murry's shapely literary creation of unwavering and unimpeachable artistic ideals, whose talents and allure seemed to grow more acute as she neared the end; or this chaotic force, one minute deep in literary creation, the next weighing up the relative merits of marmalade and golden syrup. No one gets to choose how they are remembered; and though T knew this was both inevitable and correct, it didn't stop her finding some note of tragedy in it. She wondered which version of Mansfield had more value and by what criteria it could be measured: Completeness? Verisimilitude? Beauty? Power to move? Must one self necessarily put an end to all the others?

She thought, too, of Scott's words when she announced the completion of her task: 'This is the raw material for an infinite number of investigations'; how far removed seemed 'raw' from the tidiness, the all-fair Mansfield had asked for. But then Mansfield thought we were all cannibals, devouring those we are close to. Writers especially so. 'Perhaps you will agree that we all ... absorb each other when we love,' she wrote to an aspiring novelist. 'Anatole France would say we eat each other, but perhaps nourish is the better word.'

On the train, T was turning it all over again in her mind, gazing at Mansfield's lightless eyes reflected in the window, when she remembered the pistol, how in her letters Mansfield referred to it, so teasingly.

8 October 1919, to Murry: 'I took the revolver into the garden today and practised with it: how to load and unload and fire. It terrifies me, but I feel "like a new being" now that I really can handle it and understand it. I'll never give it back.'

June 1921, to Lady Ottoline Morrell: 'On my bed at night there is a copy of Shakespeare, a copy of Chaucer, an automatic pistol and a black muslin fan. This is my whole little world.'

She had always thought it ironic that this apostle of Chekhov should mention so pointedly a revolver she never turned on herself or others. And yet, she realized now that the gun had been going off the whole time, in life and in death, and it was going off still.

.

T was puzzling over the dates again, staring at her laptop screen with her chin on her thumbs and her nose between her palms, as if in prayer. A document the archivist had sent weeks before said Annie died in 1911, so T was looking at the census record from April of that year and wondering how long she had had left then. And she wondered, again, why nobody – not her, not the archivist, not the historians – had turned up a death certificate.

Her thoughts slipped into a darker vein. Somewhere between the south and the north, she had come across the story of Blanche Monnier, a twenty-five-year-old French woman who in 1876 was locked up in a small, windowless attic room by her parents. The family – her father was called Charles – was, by all accounts, honest, bourgeois, 'nice'. Blanche's crime was her beauty and her determination to marry the man of her choice. For the next twenty-five years, the family kept her breathing, just; discovered by police after an anonymous tip-off, she was emaciated and surrounded by her own filth. The authorities told her she could live out in the world again, and, briefly, she did, before making a nuisance of herself. Doctors diagnosed her with, among many other things, exhibitionism: a desire to be seen in her entirety. In an especially cruel turn of fate, she spent the final decade of her life locked away in a psychiatric institution. Sometimes, T thought, the greatest folly of all is to trust anyone.

She knew it was outlandish, but she had started to wonder if it were possible that Annie hadn't really died in 1911, but rather had lived on longer. Perhaps not in the tower; somewhere less conspicuous. And, her mind now alive to the possibility that things were not as they had seemed and that it didn't take much for a woman to be confined against her will, other thoughts crept in through the unlatched door: what if Annie had never had tuberculosis? What if they had simply wanted to make her disappear? What if that was why, after Charles's death, the others left so hastily, stripping the house of its distinguishing features, showing no sentimentality about the family home, selling it for scrap? It wasn't merely that they didn't want to be in the house anymore; they didn't even want it to exist, as if dismembering it could undo all that had happened there.

As she hurriedly packed away her things – the train announcer had called her station, she would be there in minutes – she thought of an article she had read some years earlier, about a medieval burial site uncovered not far from those parts, where hundreds of bones were strewn across multiple pits, at some distance from the nearby church. They were, she seemed to recall, the bones of a family: a man, woman and several children. There was evidence on the bones of burning, sawing and snapping. Cannibalism was mooted and dismissed. The favourite theory was that the bodies had been scattered to guard against revenants.

But anyone who has seen a zombie film knows that that would never be the end of it.

II.

OFFCOMERS

I

Mist hung on a train platform almost unchanged since it was built it in the mid-1800s, so that it was easy to fancy mist as steam, released in great puffs from one of the old engines. T was more than a thousand feet above sea level, a sign informed her, at the highest mainline station in the land. Amid the vague grey everything – the stone of the station house, the sky and mist and rain, the mood of autumn exhaling into winter – occasional streaks of red denoted lampposts, window frames, doorways, gutters, the few details that prevented the old building from being swallowed by atmosphere. The valley beneath her and the steep climbs all around were sprayed in green and gold and oxblood.

She was on edge. It had been a long time since she last travelled alone, and since A's birth there was always the feeling of having forgotten something fundamental; how to be out in the world, how to be alone. It was nearly three in the afternoon, which was when time usually started to slip away from her, when thoughts of writing were chased out by thoughts about what kind of day A had had at nursery, what dinner she should make her, whether she would give them all the gift of a quiet night. But those thoughts seemed to belong to another person several hundred miles and other immeasurable kinds of distance from her now. She felt like Hans Castorp, the 'simple-minded but pleasant young man' of *The Magic Mountain*, arriving after two days' travel at the tiny mountain-top station, where a famous tuberculosis sanatorium awaited him. She had that sense of visiting an up-here from the down-there of her own life, and a nervous excitement bordering on fear of an unknown into which she had willingly stepped.

She was met by a taxi driver who, glancing at the

purpling clouds, ushered her quickly into his red car before jumping in himself, with a youthful nimbleness that contradicted the lines of his face. He put his flat cap on the passenger seat and his hazel eyes of yellow-ish whites caught T in the rear-view mirror.

To the inn, isn't it? he asked, and she said yes please, and they immediately settled in to talk about the weather, about the relentless rain, rivers bursting their banks, whole towns under water. Unbelievable, he said. Biblical. And she went mm-hmm and looked out of the window wondering what to say next, counting the beats of silence against hedgerow and gate. Stone walls were cast across the moors like dewy spiders' webs.

What are you up for? he asked, because he knew where her train had come from and had assumed, looking her up and down, listening to her voice, that she was of that city where the streets were paved with gold. It worried her that he should think this, that when she told him about the book, he would imagine her having come up there to pilfer what was exotic to her, to capture the lives of countryfolk like a butterfly catcher with a net, to pin them to suit her own designs. That, she thought, would be the worst. So she told him first where her day had begun, in hills not that different from these, in a place where the land met the sea, where rivers flooded and trains never came. And then she told him about her research, thinking as she said the word how ill-suited it was to Annie's case, given that no one appeared to have really searched for her before. He looked at her and said nothing, so that T wondered if he might not have heard.

Do you know the tower? she asked.

[REDACTION]? Oh yes, he said, oh yes, with a chuckle that seemed not to belong. It was built as an observatory, he said, a big eclipse he built it for, the landowner at the time, a rich gentleman, I forget his name, they were mad about all that sort of thing in those days.

And as he spoke, suddenly so fluent, she tapped into the phone nestled in her lap 'solar eclipse early 1900s' and found that none would have been visible from that spot. She did not share the information, feeling it would be somehow catastrophic to do so, that there might be no going back from the humiliation of being fact-checked like that, in real-time, and exposed, perhaps even to yourself, as a fabulist. She made interested noises so that he would continue talking.

Yes, he said, the conversation having moved into more general reminiscence, And people used to come in by train to this station here. He was pointing at a small collection of time-blackened stone buildings a little way up a hill, behind what appeared to be a timber yard.

Well, it used to be there, he said, but it was all dismantled, y'know... I remember when they came to take the track away... You'd call it a ghost station now... hundreds of them, just like it, all over the country... And there was an old bridge that came over the road just here and they took that too when they took the track because the upkeep would've been expensive, I suppose, but it's a shame, a real shame.

They were coming into the village by now, time was running out.

Do you know what happened to Annie, she said, the daughter?

He looked at her in the mirror.

Oh yes, he said, oh yes; now you mention it, I do know that story, yes, yes, she was up there, sometime after the eclipse, she lived there, yes.

He paused and looked at her again, his eyes sparking, as if a fire had just been lit behind them.

Now, *ah*, he said, I think it was... what we'd call a 'change of purpose', you see.

He smiled as he said this and made a gesture with his right hand, like a conjuror drawing a dove from the air. She nodded, gave a weak smile, said nothing.

I'm afraid I can't give you the exact dates, he said as he pulled up to the curb outside the inn and started tapping the payment into his phone screen.

She touched her phone to the reader he held out to her, said goodbye and got out of the car.

Inside the inn, in the corner by the bar, a man was balanced precariously on a milking stool, hanging tangled webs and giant black, rubbery spiders from the rough oak beams. On a table nearby a knife menaced an unblemished pumpkin.

The landlady took T's bag behind the bar so she could rush back out to get to the tower before dark. She wanted to get there before the archivist, to explore the woods where the house once stood and spend a little time alone, taking it all in, communing with the past. The landlady, who knew only that this hectic stranger was going for a walk alone in foul weather and failing light, looked on with a mixture of curiosity and concern. The wind was picking up and the rain fell hard.

I'll keep a table for you by the fire, she called as T slipped out of sight.

.

The road was the glossiest black, made pristine by fast-running water; on either side the gutters were a mulch of brown and yellow leaves, with the odd glint of silver from chocolate-bar wrappers. There were no cars, so she walked down the middle of the street to give

114

herself a better view of the buildings she passed. A pub with frosted windows, a butcher's shop, an abandoned-looking stone house with soiled lace curtains, 'Wuthering Heights' bed and breakfast. A social club advertised a gig by an Oasis tribute band called Definitely Maybe. The rain redoubled its efforts. She lowered her head and looked at her boots, half expecting them to be submerged.

The map on her phone said it was a nineteen-minute walk: straight down the road she was on, a right turn just before the bridge over the river whose rush she could already hear, and through woods that once cocooned the house. She had forty minutes at her disposal, but she kept her phone in her hand and checked it every minute or so, as if, given half the chance, space and time might decide to amuse themselves at her expense. On the right, in fields belonging to the private school, figures dressed in white and brown flowed together and apart in various formations, in pursuit of a marble-white egg. Grown men shouted after them from the sidelines. She remembered gym class, how team sports used to fill her with such dread that she would sometimes fake an asthmatic wheeze so she could stay on the bench. Running fast for short distances, as if in flight, was the only thing she had ever been any good at.

When she reached the low humped bridge, she paused to examine its arch. She had read about an old stone bridge somewhere nearby, with two intricately carved heads, one facing upstream and the other downstream to gaze at its own troubled reflection. They said the faces were there to ward off evil spirits thought to spread through the waterways, and it had reminded her of one of Rolleston's cures for tuberculous children: leave your child on a hillside near fresh water and wait for the spirits to 'end or mend them'. Had people ever done it, she wondered, or was it always just a story?

She found no carved faces, but there were two paths where she had been expecting one, both of which led into the trees. The first tended down and the second gently up, and she stared at her phone, zooming in and out of the map, looking for the pale-green dotted line that had recently denoted her path. The signal was patchy, so the map was reduced to its barest components of black water and dark green land. The tower itself had disappeared. After some deliberation she plumped for the higher of the two paths, which snaked through a field of sheep, reason having returned (the signal had not) to remind her that the tower was on a hill. As she walked, the flock parted before her, as if magnetically repelled. A couple of sheep to her left observed her until she reached the far end of the field, while the others went back to ripping at the short grass with tombstone teeth. None of them made a sound. They were a distinct local breed, those sheep, unusually large and strong, with thick coiled horns and white noses and black eyes, surrounded by a black domino mask; in the weak light, they looked like partially assembled jigsaws.

She was in the woods now, tripping over roots, skirting sturdy trunks, and it was darker than the time on her phone screen suggested it should be. The path seemed to have vanished entirely; a yellow arrow painted on a marker for walkers pointed down a sheer drop to the river, so loud it sounded like a motorway. She moved away from the edge and stepped inside a ring of large yew trees, as if for protection.

In the middle, a few short trunks were arranged on their sides around the blackened remains of a campfire, a scene that could have belonged to yesterday or to a thousand years ago, she thought, when settlers from across the sea had come ashore and followed the river

116

inland, looking for fallow land to farm. If you were to look at those lands from above, like a bird, you would see the shadows of their civilization, lying like skeletons under an emerald throw. She imagined them stopping there, under those yews, dropping bundles of meagre possessions, straightening aching backs and brushing down coarse woollen tunics with their hands, before looking about in unspoken agreement, for wood to build a fire. She saw them sheltering from weather and encroaching darkness, the firelight flickering across their tired faces and cutting luminous shapes on the tree trunks so that shadow figures darted between them. They would have told stories about themselves and others, about where they had been and where they were headed, and they would have kept an ear to the ground and a weapon nearby. A long stick, perhaps, its tip reddening in the flames, for the wolves that prowled these hills. She had no names for these travellers and could not see their faces, but she had no doubt they had been there.

Somewhere, she had read that the last wolf died about twenty miles from that spot, by the river's mouth, sometime in the fourteenth century. She turned on her phone's torch and swept the beam in a circle around herself, and it was then that she caught sight of rough stone, like tarnished silver, arching above a tangle of green. The archivist had told her to look out for these, the remains of two 'rest kiosks' – another was directly opposite – positioned at the ends of what would have been the tennis court, on the step-level below the Italianate front garden. (The land had long since rearranged itself into an undefined slope.) She felt an urge to touch stone the family might have touched or leant against between matches, sipping lemonade, but the soil all around was churned up by the tyres of some colossus, and brown water filled the

117

deep tracks. She couldn't get close.

From there, though, she could work her way around the footprint of the house with more confidence, reasoning that, where the trees were wispier, younger, where the sky was reflected in puddles, would once have been a place of polished floors. Turning on her heel, she walked back on herself and drifted through the invisible walls of the front room, whose high windows were once framed by picturesque creeper, the very same that now strangled itself on the ground. She thought of Daphne du Maurier's mournful, abandoned Manderley and of the sudden supernatural powers that lifted the narrator through locked gates 'like a spirit though the barrier'. Going deeper into the house that once was, she found amid the mud the black and white tiles of the aviary, smaller than expected and not at all in the chessboard effect she had imagined, more like a Roman mosaic of repeating geometric flowers. A little beyond these were the terracotta tiles of the back porch, edged in cream, pink and weirdly vivid turquoise. The tiles were dwindling from week to week, the archivist had said in an email, as walkers took mementos home, not knowing precisely what they were remembering, just thinking them pretty and free to claim. T stood there a moment in suspension, deliberate, covetous, then took a photograph and stepped through a doorway that was no longer there.

A narrow trench cut deep into the earth in the direction of the village, the remnants of a blind ditch used by workers coming to and from the house and gardens, designed so that the family wouldn't have to see the rough that ensured their smooth existence. From a distance the lawn would have appeared perfectly continuous, unbroken; a ha-ha, she thought, a joke of the land. The stone walls were now gauzy with moss, the ground cluttered with rotting leaves and dead, fallen branches. The wind moved through, like the last breaths of a broken body.

It had stopped raining by the time she emerged from the far end of the woods and saw the tower a little way off, bright white and gleaming glass against the inky sky. It both did and didn't feel like the first time; she had come to know the scene so well. When Freud spoke of the uncanny as a childhood belief or yearning made real in adulthood, he suggested that the returning image's power to trouble derived from its having been repressed. But, she thought, she had never forgotten the desire to make herself small enough to live inside such miniature buildings; she still felt that same pang she had as a child perusing a row of miniature China dwellings arranged on a low shelf in her grandmother's hallway. A grand stately home, a medieval mill with buckets of water drawn from a painted stream, Anne Hathaway's thatched cottage bought from a museum gift shop. She remembered how she would make a person of her hand, the index and middle finger as legs with the thumb drawing the remaining digits around the back in a gentlemanly pose, and amble from house to house, looking for a way in. She called him Doobedoo, for the ditty she sang as he walked, and he always was a man, for some reason. She summoned Doobedoo then, standing him on the upturned palm of her other hand to look at. He looked gruesome, like a hunk of meat, legs rising into a misshapen, headless body.

A house that was not a house, the unhomely as home; what must it have been like to live and die in Annie's tower? As she walked towards it, the wind pushed at her back, making a shushing noise against her raincoat and whipping hair into her eyes so she couldn't see where she was putting her feet. She was going faster than she meant to, her legs lifted and dropped by gusts from the dark wood behind. The feeling came over her that she was no longer in charge, that she had become a part of something beyond herself, with desires of its own. She thought how the word 'psyche' came from the Greek 'psykhein', meaning 'blow', because the soul-mind was as changeable as the wind.

In the weakening light, the tower looked like a lighthouse, poised on a smooth hump of mossy rock, and the land around like great rolling waves of storm and seaweed churn, in ochre and green oxide. She imagined Annie at the window, her face like a waxwork, her body a shivering mass of woollen shawls.

A voice called T's name and she turned to see a woman approaching: the archivist in a long blue coat, like an admiral. The wind dropped, just like that, as if she had commanded it. As the pair greeted each other, they gravitated to the tower's front door. A cow looked down from the upper floor – Daisy, borrowed from the 1940s and committed to cardboard by children at the primary school, the archivist explained, part of a project on local storytelling.

As the archivist wrestled with the stiff lock, T asked about the oversized antenna, like an old-style television aerial, which sprang from the side of the tower. A university not far away was conducting research, the archivist said, but she didn't know the details. Her voice bounced off featureless stone walls – they were inside by now – and only then, confronted with the blankness, did T realize that she had imagined the walls and ceilings would be covered in images or writing, like Jung's tower, strewn with motifs from a life. The air was markedly colder than outside, still and damp. If I were to lay on the tiles and stretch my arms above my head, she thought, I would touch the opposite walls with my feet at the same time.

120

The original tower had had a spiral staircase, the archivist explained, but after the incident with Daisy, they opted for a ladder. She was halfway up it as she spoke. At the ladder's top, cut into the ceiling, was a trap door, double bolted with padlocks, on the other side of which lay the relative brightness of the octagonal glass prism.

(Prism; prison – I have just now appreciated the nearness.)

Upstairs, they sat on the window ledges with their backs to the glass. The archivist seemed reluctant, T thought, to discuss Annie. Perhaps she was imagining it, but when T said the name a curious half smile seemed to play across the archivist's lips and her eyes looked as if from a distance, puzzling her out. The archivist referred to 'Evangeline Annie', said that was the name they had found in the records, what few records they had found. Not Elizabeth Annie? T asked, but the other was quite sure, and so they moved on, leaving a small hole behind, like a dropped stitch.

The archivist talked about the plans for the rebuild, said they had hoped to install a retractable roof and a telescope, to crack open this tiny space to the immensity of the celestial everything. But the money hadn't been there. They both pondered the roof in silence, imagining what might have been, and T told her the taxi driver's story of the astronomy-mad landowner and the eclipse. The archivist laughed. I haven't heard that one before, she said, But it's true that he was phenomenally rich, and possibly eccentric, living a gilded life in a poor and conservative part of the world.

T thought of the family's fantastical wealth set on a hill above the grey-stone village, of what their existence might have awakened in the minds of people who saw but could not touch. When inequality is extreme, when there is a great chasm between people, words about fur coats and any number of strange happenings pile in to level the field.

Charles ran a chain of pharmacies, the archivist said, which was very unusual at the time.

To T this was new information; she had suspected old money.

I don't know where I got it from, the archivist said, I might have made it up.

They sat for a moment in silence, unsure where to meet on such unstable ground.

Do you know about the fall? the archivist asked, finally; How they lost everything almost overnight?

The son, she said, had died on the heels of the father, leaving the widowed Alice to face double death duties, enough debt to sink the entire household. She didn't know what had killed Charles Jnr, but he would not yet have been forty.

They were on the ground floor again by now – forgive me, it is difficult to reconstruct exactly how this conversation played out – and T realized as she stepped outside, while the archivist locked the door behind them, that she had frittered away the only chance she would probably ever have to put herself in Annie's place. She hadn't checked if she could see, or hear, the river down the way or if it was hidden by the curve of the hill; or if she could spot the village church spire, whose bells would have rung out the hours of the day then as they were now. She hadn't held her head at the height of Annie's pillow to see if, first thing in the morning, she might have gazed down on the gnarled old oak squatting a little way off and summoned faces from its bark.

As they wandered back towards the woods, a crow laughed, keeping itself out of sight.

They left a different way to how T had come, veering left down a track that swept around the side of where the house once stood, dipping down beneath the roots of the trees. The old driveway, the archivist said, pointing out gravel held in place by moss, as if the plant-life had taken it on itself to preserve the final vestiges of wealth and status that had once shaped everything in sight. Mad, monstrous rhododendron and azalea bushes leered at them, brushing their arms, desperate for attention. An acer had burst into flames on the righthand side, in the shadows of Douglas firs and an enormous monkey-puzzle tree. She thought of Manderley again, silent and secret, and how nature would always come into her own in the end, her long fingers spidering, touching everything, converting all to her plan; T saw pale-limbed birches, twisted elms, ivy-choked beeches, and knew that nature had turned in on herself.

But T was walking away from Manderley, not towards it, and she was not a lonely dreamer in the moonlight of a windless night. As they reached the bottom of the driveway the four great stone pillars of the gate stood tall, proudly unsold, their spear pinnacle tops like the helmets of Prussian guards. A little further, where the track met the main road again, she stopped and looked over her shoulder. The gate posts were as defiant as the four horsemen of the apocalypse. And beyond them, on the hill, chaos.

·

Back in the village, a few brave souls moved through the wet night, trick or treating. Two girls, perhaps about ten, dressed respectively as a black cat and a ginger-haired witch T recognized from one of A's story books, marched up a cobbled lane towards a house with a plastic pumpkin lantern blinking on the doorstep. Further up the street, a diminutive demon-clown pulled a woman by her sleeve around the corner and out of sight.

A reminder chimed on T's phone, and she looked at the screen to see words she was expecting: 'Marie Bashkirtseff's death day'. A note she had set herself some time ago but needn't have, because death days, for her, had always been a bit like birthdays, known once, etched into the memory forever. She prided herself on being able to recall them. Not in a morbid way; it was more that she liked the way the act of remembering created a tentative connection between her and this other person, otherwise unknown and confined to history. That's what gave her satisfaction: the way remembrance seemed to trick the calendar and the clock for just a minute, making a past person present again, placing them in her moment, among her things, making the time of the living and of the dead one and the same for the briefest of spells. Fleeting resurrections. So, Bashkirtseff could be by her side as she walked down the street of a strange village; then she was gone again.

T came to a bus stop that had been converted into a book shelter, in which shelves crowded with old paperbacks sat beneath a notice: 'Help yourself, give it back or replace.' Among the thrillers and crime procedurals that dominated the selection, a title caught her eye: *I Am Missing*. She teased it out by the spine and read the back: 'When a young man wakes up bruised and beaten, with no memory of who he is or where he came from, the press immediately dubs him "The Lost Man."' She returned the book to its nest. It's not Annie who has forgotten who she is, she thought, crossing the road; it's everyone else.

She walked over to the other side of the street, to a

bookshop, closed, in darkness, the streetlights seeming to have taken against it. As she searched the window display, there was a faint glow of anticipation about her, a heat in the chest; her breaths were longer on the inhale. She had the feeling – frequent, familiar – that some sign might be about to break through the surface, that everything she saw was a silkscreen on the cusp of being pierced with a message from somewhere else, that there was – I guess – a reality, or some knot of meaning at least, beneath the perceived world. She called it a feeling because she was scared to be more specific; to call it hope, or delusion. Too scared to think that if nothing broke through it was because there was nothing, simply. And because she so wanted it to be true, for there to be something deeper, some kind of hidden mechanism beneath the humdrum, often something did reach through, touched her on the shoulder or laid itself across her path so she couldn't ignore it, so she had to decipher its gift – or, rather, she read it that way. And that has a truth to it, too, doesn't it?

In the window, she saw a gently dishevelled copy of May Sinclair's *Uncanny Stories*, a collection of tales from the 1920s steeped in death, the screw turns of fate and faith, and loquacious lingering spirits. In Sinclair's world a protagonist's plans will almost certainly go awry, the murdered and dismembered return, but not necessarily for revenge, the family home simmers with dread and horror. And the grimmest threat of all arises inside rather than outside the individual's mind.

I am in one of her tales, she thought, as she made her way back to the inn; I just don't know which part I'm playing.

·

In her bedroom at the inn, she set out her possessions. She had not brought much; like Hans Castorp, she did not intend to stay. Two jumpers, the three books from the train, plus a few more dragged up from the recesses of her rucksack, her laptop, a few packets of instant oats, sleeping pills. Since A she had found it so difficult to fall asleep. For Castorp's three weeks, she had just three days, although already, after little more than three hours, there was a strange sense of being on a different clock, of having covered more ground than she would have where she had come from.

This inn has been an inn for more than 500 years, the landlady had told her when she collected her bag from the bar. T didn't recall having solicited the information, and it felt somehow loaded, as if she were suspected of having designs on the place, some secret plan to buy it and convert it into luxury holiday homes. As if it were a warning that the building itself might rebel. As if the dimples in the thick plaster of the walls might be signs of peaceless lives beneath the surface, the mute mouths of half-a-millenium's souls, opening and closing, opening. And she thought, again, as she unpacked her things, of Benjamin's essay on storytelling and his observation that, 'There used to be no house, hardly a room, in which someone had not once died,' how with each death a window was opened onto the eternal and kept ajar by stories told about the departed, stories of 'real life' that only assumed transmissible form with that final breath. 'This,' Benjamin said, 'is the stuff that stories are made of'; for the storyteller borrows his authority from death.

How many had died in her room, she wondered. How many openings into all-time could a place take before its walls would start to crumble, and cease to be present – *of* the present – at all? She didn't put her things in the wardrobe, it seemed an imposition, too permanent, instead leaving everything where she could see it, as if she might have to run in the night.

The room was small. Tiny, even. An L-shape with the downward strike taken up by the length of the single bed, and the base line made up by a shower cubicle, toilet and sink behind a thin partition wall. A desk sat at the L's kink, every inch of its surface required for the kettle, mug, tray of tea bags, sugar sachets and long-life milk pots. Within minutes of arriving, she had sent her husband a film, so he knew where to picture her, in a space as big as my hand.

Now, she wedged herself between the bed and the wall, knees bent to her chin like a child, her back against the radiator. Her laptop was on the bed as if it were a desk, and above that was the window. On the sill were a redundant flowery water jug and a potted succulent. When she had first seen it, she couldn't tell if the plant was real – its stems were so straight; even the delicate spots of decay appeared painted – so she stuck her thumbnail in until a thin translucent liquid seeped from the wound. Outside, she could just about make out the hump-backed ridge, Vantablack against plain old black, a giant glacial formation of slate and gritstone beaten by weather and time. It towered over the village.

She looked again at a photograph of the house, sent a while back by the archivist, in which, through the majestic gateposts, you could see the sweeping gravel drive gleaming white in the bright light of day, fringed by the tidiest lawn and shrubs like chocolate truffles. Above it was the house, and she didn't know how – really, she couldn't explain how on earth she'd missed it – but she realized then that the photographer had captured some activity at the largest front window, in what was probably the drawing room. A figure, a woman, she was sure, was leaning towards the glass, one arm extended, pushing back the drapes. Her head was turned to the side – it was the whiteness of her cheek that caught the eye – and she was looking out through the window. That's all. She was just there. Present, simply.

And all the while, the church bells across the street from the inn pealed as if life depended on it, and they were deafening, reverberating in T's bones so that she couldn't join thought to thought. All words were drowned out and there was only feeling, inchoate and intrusive. It was after six o'clock and she couldn't have said how long the bells had been ringing; they must have started on the hour, but somehow it hadn't registered. They might have been ringing 500 years.

.

Downstairs, the pub was virtually empty, but the landlady had made good on her promise of a table beside the fire. T couldn't feel heat in the flames, so she took a seat in the far corner of the room instead, close to the bar, where three men, probably in their fifties, perched on stools, a pint of creamy amber ale set before each. A family of grotesque spiders hung above them. After a few minutes she went to the bar. She didn't look at the men but felt their eyes on her; their murmuring had stopped. She wanted to smile and say hello, to be that person, but couldn't. She ordered a vegetarian lasagna and a pint of beer the colour of strong black tea and retreated to her corner.

She had brought Mansfield, more as a prop than for company – she would only be pretending to read – but in the end, the pull of her phone was stronger. She looked at photographs of A, scrolling back and forth through the months with a flick of the finger. There she was that morning before T left, covered in porridge, waving her spoon like a wand to magic up more, more and more; there, as a wrinkled new-born, puce and fragile, so alert, so thirsty for life from her first breath. Her husband had sent several more pictures that afternoon to reassure her that all was well and life went on without her, which both comforted and saddened her. She set a new screensaver: A, in her favourite red cardigan, standing beside the wolf, her face barely level with his, holding his lead, pulling him towards her, utterly unafraid. (The wolf, looking askew at the camera, seems to ask, Are we OK with this arrangement?)

When the lasagna arrived, she was turning Mansfield's pages as if absorbed, and listening to the men talk. They all worked at the school, she inferred, and one of them had been in the fields she passed on the way to the tower earlier, shouting at the kids. He was unhappy with their fitness levels; just back from holidays, they were not taking the game seriously. The men discussed sport of all sorts, leapfrogging from one to the next, equally invested. What would they have talked about in the days before multi-channel sports packages, she wondered; would they have shared stories of their own exploits and experiences? And if there were none to share, might they have invented something to pass the time, tall tales to keep each other entertained? She went back to the bar, taking her empty glass, a ring of foam marking every gulp, and asked for another drink. She coughed, the remnants of recent illness, but also just to make a noise, to see if she could, and the men looked at her again. The man closest to her pulled his coat over his shoulders, said goodbye, and made for the door. She coughed again. Don't worry, she said, I'm not infectious. A laugh escaped her, though nothing was funny.

She ordered a half pint of the same, and one of the two remaining men asked her what she thought of the beer. It was delicious – too delicious, she said, pointing at the half-measure; I'm pacing myself. They don't make it like this down south, she said, knowing what they wanted to hear, knowing how to ingratiate herself and thinking it worth her while.

Then the inevitable question: What're you up for?

She told them she was researching a book, and she thought how it got easier to say the line every time, but also harder, realer, less of an act.

Have you written other books, before this one? the first man asked, which seemed an abrupt follow-up, she thought, as if he were trying to catch her out, expose a fraud. She answered yes, she had.

And so, if someone were to ask you what you do, he continued, y'know, what you *are*, what would you say? Would you say, 'I'm an author'?

She said she hadn't really thought about it (a lie), but, yes, she supposed she would.

And what's your book about, he asked.

She told him it was about the tower.

The tower? the men said, in unison.

The [REDACTED], she said.

Right, said the first man. And what are you writing about it then?

She said that she was interested in what had happened there, or what people thought had happened there, but did not say what in particular because she felt it would have been like leading the witness, getting them to say something they didn't really believe until they believed it with all their heart. But because they said nothing, just looked at her, she kept talking. I suppose, she said – because in the brief time she had been up there she had felt her footing shift – it's also about stories, about why some take hold of us (she made two tight fists and shook them) and others don't.

Right, said the first, while the second took a long drink.

She asked them what stories they knew about the tower, and the men looked at each other, then away again quickly. Nervously, she thought, as if wishing to confer before committing themselves. She sensed the landlady behind the oak-panelled wall of the back bar, keeping herself out of sight.

Do you mean about the girl? said the first.

Annie, she said.

Was that her name?

She nodded.

That she had smallpox, you mean?

Tuberculosis, she said. She died there after three years.

Oh, said the first, I never knew she died there.

I don't know anything about all that, said the second. And I've been here all my life. I just know that there's a tower on the hill and it's been there as long I have and then some. I don't know about the rest of it, I don't know about a dead girl.

The first man and T looked at the second man, waiting for him to say something else, to honour the rule of storytelling: that if you take a story away, you must leave something in its place. 'Help yourself, give it back or replace.' But the second man seemed anxious now, fiddling with the zip of his black sports coat. He finished his pint and said he was off to the social club across the road. You coming? he said, and she realized he was talking to her as much as to his friend.

If you want to talk to *real* locals, said the first, as he got his coat, you'd best come along.

131

('Real' locals? she thought; had they been pretending all this time?)

The landlady peered around the corner, wiping a clouded glass with an old rag, making it cloudier, and watched her go.

The social club turned out to be a sports club, with several screens showing football, cricket, snooker. The decorations were a peculiar mixture of fairy lights, sports memorabilia, and the ubiquitous fake cobwebs. A cold tinge to the spotlights in the ceiling made her feel like she was in a fish tank. The first man ordered a round of drinks and took it on himself to introduce her to people.

You'll be all right if you're with me, he said. Some can be a bit funny about offcomers.

Offcomers? she said.

Not from here, said the second man, Strangers.

Offcomers had wandered off the moors or followed the river's path inland since time began, T thought. They had come here, to these people, asking for something, always asking, or not asking but taking anyway. And before there were people to receive the requests, they took what they found.

Here, he said, to anyone who walked past, Meet my friend, she's an author. They had swapped names but did not use them, as if embarrassed or afraid of the intimacy.

The club was busy.

Tuesday nights are always like this, the first man said. Brass band, bell ringers, firefighters – everyone comes after practice.

Was *that* what that was, she said, pointing out of the window at the church tower.

He nodded.

I thought it was for Halloween, she said, sheepish. To mark the start of the three days of the dead. Her

132

disappointment was visible, and he laughed and shook his head.

Come here and meet this author, he said again, hooking his arm around a woman's shoulders, like a shepherd with his crook. She's writing a book, you have to talk to her, she needs *real* locals.

Some stopped, others slipped his grip and headed to the back of the room, closer to the screens. To those who stopped, turning their faces on her like lamps, T swallowed her embarrassment as best she could and explained again about the tower and the stories, those that gripped you and those that didn't.

You must be a very intelligent woman, said the second man. To write books. He looked at her in wonder, as if she might transform into a beast before his very eyes.

Not at all, she said, I just can't get a real job.

Everyone laughed, even the people with their backs turned, watching men in a place where it was daytime kick a ball across an impossibly green field. She had said what the people were thinking and wanted to hear spoken aloud, and it was better that way, she thought, better that she had anticipated their thoughts, that they were laughing with her.

I used to go up there picking blackberries with my sisters, said one man, who must have been about sixty, with tight curls in silver and slate. It was just ruins then, good for hide and seek and not much else. It was full of graffiti, last I heard, said another man, behind her. Just after they'd done it all up, it was open, no door on the thing, and immediately it was vandalized, would you believe it? Who'd do a thing like that? said the barman. No one from around here, that's for sure, said a woman as she squeezed past with a tray of liquorice-black beers.

She asked about Annie; didn't anyone know her story?

Weren't they scared to go up there as children, to play hide and seek where someone had died in such tragic circumstances? Didn't it creep you out? she asked.

I don't know that I knew that story at the time, said the curly haired man. But I know it now – not that it's true, like, or that it isn't, but I do know it, yes.

There was a fire up there, a quiet voice from somewhere behind T said, and everything was –

But another voice interrupted to say: I knew about the girl.

It was a woman in her thirties who spoke now, a firefighter, oddly enough, still in her uniform, as if the word 'fire' had summoned her. But there were so many stories, she said, so many... It was ruins, y'know, nothing there, she said, so us kids could just make up whatever we wanted: that the mosaics were from a Roman temple, that the tower was a pillbox from the war, or all that was left of a medieval castle. You could say anything, she said, and you'd believe it yourself.

T could see how that might happen.

Did someone say there was a fire? she asked, but whoever had spoken the words had now gone or was unwilling to speak up again and those who stood around shrugged their shoulders or shook their heads blankly.

Most people wanted to tell her about Daisy the cow, and this was funny, she thought, because Daisy got stuck in the 1940s, before anyone in that room had been born. And yet that was the story that held them; that was the story they told so vividly, as if they had seen it with their own eyes.

She got stuck up there did poor Daisy, they said, took five strong men with winches to pull her out.

And then the firefighter told a story about her first day on duty, when she took a call about a cow in a tree and she thought it must be some kind of joke, but when she arrived at the scene – lo and behold – there was a cow suspended in the branches of an oak.

But how did she get there? T asked.

After a period of prolonged rain, the river had risen so high that the animal had been swept up by the current and caught in overhanging branches. It was quite a job to get her feet back on the ground, the firefighter said.

Another drink had magicked its way into T's hand by now and though she protested that it had been her round to buy her chaperone was unpersuadable. She had stopped asking about Annie, stopped insisting that everyone remember what they wanted to forget or may never have known, and the conversation moved on to other things: to the school and how it seemed to employ everybody in the town, one way or another, and how it looked after some but others less so. Several people nodded and mm-hmmed in agreement. One man finished his drink quickly and walked away. The village had become very expensive, they said. Hmm. No one, no locals, could afford the houses anymore. Mm-hmm. Parents from outside the village bought second homes there, to fiddle the rules and get their child into the school's catchment area, so they could pay lower fees. And these people were the worst. Hmm.

Offcomers? she said, and people laughed at the same time as they nodded.

The second man, from the inn, had vanished without a word, she noticed, and she asked the first man if he would be back. She owed him a drink, too.

Oh, no, he's had his fill, said the first man, swirling the dregs in his glass. He knows when to call it a night, he said, looking her straight in the face for what felt like the first time.

.

In bed, with the lights off and the covers drawn up to her chin like a child in a film, she ran through the evening, trying to piece it together from start to finish but losing her way, trying to work out what had been gained from speaking to strangers. Amid a carnival of faces and voices, she kept picturing the cow in the tree, then the cow in the tower, and it was so ridiculous, she thought, that that had been the thing that stuck. And when she tried to go back, to picture Annie in the tower, or even herself sitting there earlier that day with her back to the window, it was as if something had broken, or – actually – more like something had been stolen and replaced with something completely different, pointless, like – I don't know – a pencil swapped for a carrot. A substitution was being attempted, she thought, one story pushed out by another, a tragedy replaced with a comedy. She would resist it.

So, she closed her eyes and took herself back to the tower. Alone, she drifted through the gateless gateposts and up the misty once-white driveway, past the stone arches black with rain, until she found herself among trees so closely, lightlessly, packed that their trunks appeared carved from one block. In the foreground, a plumb tree, the only surviving member of its family, dropped a final leaf, silver, tear-like, and stood resigned. Everything was tangled in ivy and brambles, a suffocating weave of life out of control. Overhead, branches clacked against each other in the wind, like a dog gnashing its teeth. She conjured up a world of sadness and foreboding, of doom and decay and then she lay with it, reassured, wrapped around in clean white sheets.

As she moved through the woods towards the tower, shadow figures in thick fur coats, part-woman-part-bear,

136

prowled the perimeter of their territory. They were off-comers, she thought; rich offcomers, the worst, and how unwelcome had they been? She felt heat on her back and turned to see flames dancing among the trees, licking at the ghostly walls of the old house.

Beyond, on the hill, Annie's prison was restored to ruin, and she thought how much better it was that way, how you could say whatever you wanted when it looked like that. She saw its yawning doorway, unfathomable again, the stone walls grey and rough, stripped of genteel white plaster; a few glinting shards of glass suspended from thin, rotten frames were all that remained of the top floor. The wind shrieked through, its belly sliced. She thought of the deck of tarot cards she had bought as a teenager, how she had never learnt to read them properly because she feared what they might tell her. She spent hours in the attic admiring the ornate, macabre pictures, arranging them in suggestive scenarios, then jumbling them again in a panic. They said it was the card of misery, the tower, the card of danger and deception, that it warned of unexpected disaster.

The invisible crow wasn't laughing, she made sure of that, and though she tried to imagine the call of an owl or the howl of a wolf instead, nothing came. She was tired and the bed was warm; to think of anything else seemed impossible. And as she slipped towards sleep, it was as if the scene she had made in her mind were stretching, growing thinner and thinner, tearing, until it simply wasn't there, and now her feet were treading air and all she could hear was a curious, distant moan, like the lowing of a fearful cow.

137

¶ *There is a spider in the corner of the room, against the window. She wasn't there yesterday. I expect she has come in to shelter from the rain, and I don't mind, I like the company. I watched her make her web this morning, and when she was done, I put a tiny piece of paper in its centre, the corner of this page in fact. I suppose I just wanted her to know I was there and that I was allowing her to live in my home. She came to investigate, looked at it from all angles, and then, apparently judging it worthless, returned to the corner. I would like to remove the paper now but I am scared that I'll damage the web. So I'm sort of split, you see, between two impulses: the one, to draw a line under the business, to ask the spider's forgiveness and hope my actions haven't inconvenienced her too greatly; and the other, to rip it out, to destroy her and the web, not to be reminded of this insufferable need of mine to be seen, and to have power over something, anything at all.*

II.

She woke up with a foggy head, the sound of her heart squerching inside it, and though I say 'woke up', we can't be sure she was ever really asleep. Alcohol affected her that way now, another change since A. Where once drink used to sink her into a sleep so deep she remembered no dreams, nothing, in the morning, now it held her at the surface, keeping her awake for hours; or if not fully awake then in that slightly dipped place, where you are aware of dreaming at the same time as you believe the strange visions to be absolutely tangible and the most illogical thoughts take on granite-like rationality. Held there, her nerves searched every corner for the embers of anxieties to rekindle. In the night, several times, she had heard the cries of a baby and though she knew it wasn't real – or knew it wasn't there, then – still she sat upright and swept the room with the light of her phone screen, like an exorcist clutching a crucifix. When A was very new T's brain had played this trick often. She would recognize A's cry in the shriek of the gull nesting on a neighbours' roof or the scream of a fox, and burst into the nursery, sharpened to a spike, electrified, ready to give herself completely. A, who had been sleeping soundly until that moment, would wake with a start and then she really would cry, and the universe laughed.

After a pot of instant porridge in her room, T slipped out of the side door into the street, stopping briefly to zip her coat against a hoarse wind. A crow peeped down from the gutter, his eyes like polished jet. It was market day, on the same day it had been for ever, and a few stalls were arranged in a car park, selling local honey, bread, cheese, red meat. She hovered close enough to scrutinize the quality of some croissants and to ascertain that cashless payment would be possible, but not so close as to commit. The baker greeted a man behind her as if she weren't there. 'Now then,' he said. 'Now then,' said the other, and it seemed to her the perfect formulation for this place of change and constancy, where cash had become invisible and words five centuries old still circulated.

It was cold outside, colder than the previous day, and her fists retracted into the sleeves of her puffa jacket like the heads of startled tortoises. As she made her way to the tower, sometimes breaking into a run to try to warm up, and because of a nervousness she preferred to exhaust than explain, she remembered that Mansfield had found the cold frightening, 'ominous'. 'I breathe it and deep down it's as though a knife softly softly pressed in my bosom and said "Don't be too sure."' She knew it would not take much to end her. 'That is the fearful part of having been near death,' she said. 'One knows how easy it is to die. The barriers that are up for everybody else are down for you and you've only to slip through.' T had sighed when she read those words, *having been*; as if, when she wrote them, death were not still at Mansfield's shoulder, poised to cut. Beneath the high-low cycle of hope and disillusion, the tall tales of miracle treatments and curative climes, the sharpest edge of reality was always there. She wondered if Mansfield had known that her own words were make-believe, one more mask among the many, only held up to herself this time, like when you look at your own tear-stained face in the mirror and tell yourself everything will be all right.

She asked herself if Annie had thought she was getting better, that her father's regime was working; if, having lived three years alone in a glass prism, 'better' was something she felt she could ever truly be. What would it have meant, after all, to be healed; to take deep, painless breaths? To cough without fear and everyone's eyes immediately on her? To go back to the big house and – I don't know – feel like her old self again, take up her life of embroidery and scrapbooks, her seat at the piano? To marry? Have children? Did she dare to dream beyond what was prescribed for her sex and class? Could she have been the historians' exception? These questions and others like them fluttered about T's mind like confetti, a cheap diversion from her essential doubt that healing was ever possible with a knife inside you. She thought of Mann, for whom illness was only the beginning, an 'initiation' to death, a 'necessary passage' to a higher plane of understanding: the 'genius way'. But none of his characters ever did make it out the other side.

The rain came horizontally, running down the right side of her face and tracing the curve of her jaw, like a cold finger. She stopped – picture her at the tower now, breathless, hot blood pumping with conviction – and looked up at the windows' perfect reflection of turbulent clouds, thinking how the sky seemed somehow more tangible, more like itself, for being framed. Except: didn't the glass also look like water, she thought, stirred by wind? And once her mind had observed it, as with an inkblot, she could see only that, each watery window becoming a site of scrutiny, as if something vital might bubble up from its depths.

She hadn't come for the tower that day, though, and she tore herself away, carrying on through the woods, downhill, emerging on the other side into a wide meadow, where the wind was weaker and her thoughts calmer. She was looking for the ancient oak tree that had given the estate its name. A photograph on her phone showed its relation to the old house, so that she was able to locate it using the stone arches as guides. It stood apart from the wood by quite some way, which partly explained why she had missed it the previous day; that, and the fact she had been expecting something massive, majestic and – well – unmissable. The reality was a stocky mass, easy to overlook, your eye drawn by the arterial red of a nearby beech. She would probably have missed it again, said to herself with confidence that this could surely not be the one, had she not happened to speak to a friend on the phone the previous night, a farmer's daughter, who knew more about the land than T knew about anything. A tree that old will be wide not tall, she had said, explaining how, according to the old ways, its limbs would have been cut or snapped each summer to make tree hay, a tangle of twigs clinging to leaves, the farmer's wager against the cold wet summers that wrecked the meadow crop. A tree was rarely allowed to grow much higher than the man who tended it, she said, it was his shadow in that sense, and if he knew what he was doing it would force the tree to drive her roots deeper into the earth, so that in times of drought, when other plants died, it soldiered on.

That great survivor had outlived every man that touched it by hundreds of years, and now its neglected branches like long tired arms rasped against the ground in the wind, scratching its tale into the earth with tapered fingers. A noise somewhere between a whine and a creak resonated from its crooked, callused chest. But still, it had not given up: vibrant green sprang up beside deadwood, and in places, rock-like bark had peeled away to reveal a smoother texture, like the grooved throat of a beached blue whale.

They used to say the oak was the first tree created by the gods, that all men leapt fully fleshed from there. And if someone couldn't believe that then perhaps they could believe that Dryads, whose name meant 'oak', concealed themselves in the trees' hollow spaces, living so long as there were new buds in spring. T remembered how one winter when she was a child, a neighbour, raking dead leaves from the lawn, plucked an oak leaf and let it go above her head so she could catch it as it drifted down, for her good health. Carry an acorn in your pocket and you'll be well while the days are short; burn oak to warm your house and lingering sickness will fly up the chimney – you will have heard these, too, I'm sure, only some of the things they used to say, and perhaps still do somewhere. Always the oak has provided hope where otherwise there might have been none. She had read that morning that the Sanskrit 'Duir', meaning 'oak', had given rise to the English 'door', and maybe, she thought, that was why the tree was associated with a passage from darkness to light. She stood there waiting, feeling nothing but the cold rising through the soles of her feet.

The rain was showing real intent now, there seemed to be more water than air, so she took refuge in the wood, under the dense canopy of deciduous firs and yews. They used to hang poachers from trees, she thought, her mind now open to the lore of old. Not these trees, probably. But once she had thought it, she couldn't shake the image of men dangling by their necks, like moles wrenched from the earth by a catcher and strung from a gate.

As she moved through the wood, she trod the underlying narrative.

Why were poachers put to death?

Because they took what was not theirs to take.

She heard the invisible crow laugh. Or she thought she did.

•

The antenna beside the tower – until this point she, too, was in the dark – was there to observe the activity of a rare songbird called the white-throated dipper, a small but sturdy species, named for the way it dipped its head beneath the surface of the fast-flowing river that is its natural, and only, habitat. The ecologist responsible for the study (she had spoken to him on the phone that morning) described a rigorous process of tagging and monitoring, with real-time tracking and minute-by-minute signals pinging off nodes and masts spanning three or four valleys. The data was being harvested, he said, sent to a cloud.

The ecologist wanted to know how each bird moved around between birth and death, to understand how the changing life of the river changed the lives of these birds, its ancient dependents. Dippers would never leave the water's side, he said, because they took all their food from the riverbed, so the life of a dipper was one with the life of its river: poison the water and the dipper was poisoned; if the river dried out, the dipper starved; if it ran too deep and fast, again, the dipper starved. Or its nest, built on low hanging branches, close to the water's surface, would flood or be swept away. You will never find a dead dipper, the ecologist said, because the water always claims it in the end.

The river was raging now; you could hear it from the town. T had come back to her room to dry her socks and had become absorbed in the plight of this curious bird that flouted the distinction between the world above water and the world beneath its mirror face, whirring through the air one minute, plunging headfirst into the spume the next. The dipper's wings were muscular, she read, more like the flippers of a penguin than the delicate fans of its cousin, the thrush. Gliding through the water, black-brown feathers, coated in air, gleamed like the platinum scales of a bream. She found audio clips of the dipper's song and its short, repetitive peep-peep, its throaty intermittent chirrup, sounded, she thought, like the internet dial-up tone of the olden days. The dippers that flitted above the water now – she had seen none but the ecologist assured her they were there – must be the descendants of dippers that had flitted above the water in Annie's time, she thought, and the notion was satisfying, as resilience often is, proof of a will uncowed by fate.

That morning, between finding the old oak and returning to the inn, she had gone back to the tower; like a finger probing a scab, she couldn't keep away. And as she stood back, squinting into the rain, she had noticed for the first time a CCTV camera positioned just under the pitch of the roof, its black swivelling intelligence trained on her. A response, she presumed, to the vandalism mentioned at the social club.

It unsettled her to know that she was being watched in anticipation of some crime she might commit, or already had, that she had been filmed the previous day and would be the next. She imagined her past, present and future selves being digitized, atomized, harvested and stored in a cloud. There was an authority above her, always; how foolish to have forgotten. As she moved around the tower, transformed now into the central well of a panopticon, she felt exposed and embarrassed. Self-awareness distorted her thoughts, as if she were cross-examining herself, as if she had been taken out of her own body to observe from the outside, from above. She saw a woman, an author, tiny and lost.

She remembered how Jung had felt observed by his tower, how daydreaming one day, an eye had appeared to him in the dappled stone. He took up his tools and, at the

eye's centre, chiselled a miniature homunculus, the figure of himself, a 'little doll', caught in the pupil of another's eye. The figure emerging from the stone was Telesphorus of Asklepios, an ancient Greek god of healing, with his hooded cloak and a lantern, pointing the way across the vast landscape that separates the well from the unwell; he represented recovery, a coming out on the other side. All this Jung seemed to know instinctively, as if the day's events had occurred before, perhaps many times, and he was piecing things together from memories.

Had T been expecting some kind of revelation at Annie's tower? Yes, I think she had, although she hadn't dared to admit it to herself, nor commit it to the page. But it's true that she believed certain things, extraordinary things, could happen when you were immersed in a place, breathing its air, watching the interplay of light and shadow, and when she had imagined herself up there beside the tower, her faith in the extraordinary had swelled, eclipsing reason, imposing its own logic. Through close observation, she had thought, by picking out timeless things that Annie too must have observed – like how the skin of the birches on the edge of the wood grew paler, luminescent, moments before nightfall; or how a female squirrel, driven to the end of her branch by a male, lunged and clicked her teeth like a bareknuckle fighter – a kind of rupture could be made in time, so that past and present would bleed into each other. And, so long as those birches stood and the squirrels proliferated, the future would join them too, and a rich continuity would be born. It was only the same kind of fantastical thinking that had made her imagine that a surgeon's blade could slice through layers of time to reveal something essential, something that might allow one woman's life to open into another's, like kissing mouths.

When she felt the tower's eye on her, it came into focus: the lengths to which she had gone, the pressure she had applied, the blind spots and silences she had ignored. A knot in her stomach tightened, and she knew it had been there all along, the result of a conflict she had never known how to resolve, between what she imagined, or wished, and what was. She remembered how, one day, when a friend had asked her if Annie's story wasn't just an old tale got out of hand, she had heard a voice inside her say *maybe, yes, probably*, and she had recoiled as if from a loaded gun, falling back into the tragedy with a capital T, the injustice, the betrayal, working it all over again until she felt reassured. She remembered the softness in her friend's voice, realized now that the pity had not been for Annie.

.

She was standing outside the History Society, an unassuming building of the same stone as everything else in the village, waiting for the woman from the tourist information office to key in the door code and let her inside. She rubbed her hands together and stamped her feet, more the performance of being cold than an accurate reflection of temperature. Her eye wandered across the street while she waited, coming to rest on the familiar red, blue and white 'T' of a dead-end sign. A cobbled lane to nowhere, its name set on another sign in black and white: The Folly. The first note of a laugh escaped her, which she disguised as three short coughs.

Inside, the woman from tourist information said the historian was waiting, and she pointed to an otherwise undistinguished white door, at the end of the corridor. She watched as T reached her destination, then she disappeared.

149

The historian sat at a table with three thick yellow folders arranged neatly in front of him, like the lit windows of a house at night. All around were colour-coded files, shelf above shelf, from floor to ceiling, of red, yellow and green, a traffic-light system of information. The worn grey carpet was covered in boxes of all sizes and condition, each with a different name scribbled in someone else's hand.

When people die, he said, weary, apologetic, their families bring us their things to sort.

He gestured to a chair beside him, the kind she remembered from school, whose tilted plywood seats slid you into place and snagged your tights whenever you stood. She sat down. A square tin in front of her, with a slot cut in the top 'For Donations', was difficult to ignore. She folded up the emergency £10 she kept in her wallet and posted it through as the historian looked studiously away, busying himself with one of the folders.

He asked what her connection was with that corner of the world – Most people turn left before they get here, he said – and she told him she had none, nothing more than an interest in Annie and her family, which he knew already from their emails. Nothing more than a feeling, she said.

Inside the first folder were photocopies of the auction brochure for the house; an agreement signed by a local firm and the school governors for its demolition; and four or five printouts of the same thing, the local newspaper story of the cow who got stuck in the tower. A cartoon, unsigned, recreated the scene, casting Daisy as Rapunzel, letting down her hair.

In the second folder was a potted history of the house giddily describing Charles's renovations:

there were turrets, wings, extensive gardens and driveways and gateways, a ha-ha and an orangery: inside it was beautifully and expensively furnished and decorated. The Misses dressed in the height of fashion and "always wore fur coats". Invitations to the "big house" were rare!

The quotations within the quotation struck her, how those words, cordoned off from the rest, could have been borrowed from an original statement made by someone in particular – an authority, one of the housekeepers, say – or could belong to a faceless mass of whispering villagers and so, in effect, to nobody verifiable at all.

A short notice from the mid-1990s in the parish newsletter suggested the 'spicey possibility' that the tower be rebuilt from ruin (a possibility that didn't become reality for some twenty years), and told of poor 'Anne who sadly at the age of 18 developed Tuberculosis and had to live in isolation there till she died aged only 21.'

Another document, typed on plain paper, mentioned a night in 1936, when the house 'burnt down mysteriously', but this was struck through in blue biro, the words 'was demolished' written in the margins, not once but twice, as if in frustration at a rumour that refused to die.

In the third folder, she found a health report, nearly thirty years old, for the oak tree: even back then its condition was assessed as 'very poor'. Its seeding date, based on its girth and heavily burred and pollarded appearance, was given as *c.* 1330. Its branches had 'antlered', the report noted, and she imagined a time when the tree's transformation would be complete: one quiet morning, it would spring from the soil and, with knotted roots for legs, take off; a stag, lord of the woods, dancing across the land.

She told the historian that she had found the oak that morning, that it had been much lower to the ground than expected; that, if the report's date was correct, that tree had witnessed more than they could ever imagine. Who knows, she said, it might have seen the last wolf scream by, pursued by men and dogs. The historian looked at her but said nothing.

They say the last wolf died not far from here, she said.

People say the last wolf died wherever they want the last wolf to have died, he replied, turning back to the shelves.

Behind the oak's report was a photograph of two women, both with broad smiles standing in front of the tower. From the style of their summer dresses and pin curls, T thought it must be some time in the 1950s. She had seen one of the women before, among the documents the archivist had sent months earlier. She asked the historian if he knew her identity, and he said she was a woman who 'concerned herself' with local history, dead now. He paused and looked at T, a gauging kind of look. But, he said, she was more of a writer than a historian, if you know what I mean.

It was not a question, but she felt she did know what he meant: that this woman was someone like her. To change the subject as much as anything else, she asked him if he knew why the lane across from them – she pointed at it through the window – was called The Folly. He looked at her again with something like suspicion on his face now, as if it were a trick question, and said, slowly, that he did not. But you might find something in here, he said, passing her a book by the writer-not-historian and returning to the shelves behind her, in search of records relating to Annie.

Strange characters, 'real locals', spilled from the pages: a Bird Man, who for decades imported from the mountains of some faraway land, rare, golden singing canaries famed for their uncanny ability to imitate musical instruments; a sword-dancing man who told wild stories of killing the fairies that 'infested' the hills all around the village; and a man who lived more than 140 years. And she read, too, of the 'famous' woman who sat at the top of the cobbled lane called The Folly, knitting from dawn to dusk, looping yarn over yarn and never dropping a stitch, tightening each with determination, hundreds of tiny nooses in a row.

The historian interrupted her reading by placing a red folder on the table, open to a page showing the baptismal records of the church down the road, opposite the inn. And there, beside his finger, was 'Elizabeth Annie', baptized 28 August 1889. She was underwhelmed by the information but thanked him. It confirmed which of the two birth certificates was real, but the death certificate continued to evade them all, she said. He suggested they check the parish burial records under the family's surname and pulled another red folder from the shelf. There, they found Annie's mother Alice, dead in 1937, at the age of eighty-three, and T remembered what the archivist had said about the double duties after the deaths of husband and son in quick succession, that the fall had been sudden and dramatic. She wondered if, in her advanced age, the grief and the burden had finished Alice off. A year later her house would be torn to pieces; at least she didn't live to see it.

But the historian's finger had travelled down the page ahead of her eyes and was pointing now at the record for Charles Jnr, who died, the record said, thirty-odd years after his mother, in 1971, at the age of eighty-six. She asked herself whether, until now, anything she had learnt since arriving in the village was true; fact and fiction seemed to tip into each other so eagerly up there.

Still though, there was no sign of Annie, and T took it as a kind of validation, proof that it was not for lack of effort or diligence, or any other failing on her part, that Annie had not been found so far.

She didn't die here, she said. If she had, her name would be on this list, wouldn't it?

She spoke like a girl asking the teacher to explain why the sums didn't add up as they should.

I might have something for you there, said the historian; and she felt the muscles in her back tense as if her wings were readying themselves for flight.

He had been at the church earlier that day, at a regular coffee morning enjoyed by the parish elderly, and there got talking to the undertaker, who sketched for him, by memory, across a series of paper scraps, an elaborate diagram of heredity. Now, the historian unfolded page after page before her, smoothing each on the table and bringing them together like the pieces of a puzzle. Lines in black biro scalloped from name to name, forming a complicated web of union, generation, obligation and disappointment.

According to this, said the historian, Annie didn't die when you think she did. He pointed at her name – Elizabeth Annie ('Bessie') – then traced with his finger the black lines that emanated from it: She married and had children, he said without emotion. Around the time of her supposed death, she had shed her family's surname like an old skin and grown a new one.

Oblivious to the blow he had dealt T, he went back to the files on the wall to look for a burial record attached to the marital name. He pulled down another red folder and flipped back and forth through the pages.

And that is where they found her, almost too easily, under her husband's name: She died in 1977, the record said, at the age of eighty-seven.

Done, said the historian, rapping a knuckle on the table.

He began to clear things away, returning files to their correct, colour-coded places. It was time for T to leave, according to the grammar of his movements. Done.

Done!

Strange glee. She took a photograph of the burial record before it disappeared again and lassoed Annie's name in blue with a wand-like wave of her finger.

.

It was late afternoon when she walked back to the inn. The wind had strengthened again, coming in sporadic gusts that bullied her from behind. The rain didn't fall but was fired like a hail of arrows.

In her bedroom she sat on the bed, her legs tucked underneath her. Her face was hot, her hands as cold and white as marble. Was it possible to experience relief and disappointment at the same time? Relief at the thought that Annie might have lived a full and happy life; disappointment at the loss of something meaningful. She pulled her phone from the back pocket of her jeans and in its saved numbers tapped 'Undertaker'. The historian had phoned her minutes after she had left his office to say that the men had just spoken and the undertaker was willing to be contacted.

He knew who she was as soon as she spoke, had been expecting her call. She wondered what the historian had told him about her. That she was more of a writer than a historian, if you know what I mean.

I don't know that I'll be able to tell you much that you don't already know, he said, and she replied that she thought he probably would because it seemed increasingly likely that what she thought she knew was little more than a web of hearsay cast down the decades. He explained that his information came by way of his grandfather, who had worked on one of the farms owned by the family into which Annie had married, in – he thought – 1913.

I don't know if you know about the daughters? he said, That they eloped, both of them, ran away and married?

Annie, too? she said.

If that's her name, yes, he said, two of them eloped, sisters, if you'd believe it, a terrible ruckus it caused.

He said it as if it had just happened, as if he himself had been inconvenienced by the affair. He said he would have to do some digging for the details, that if she gave him her email address, he would send her everything he knew.

Were there children? she asked, as if she had not already seen them recorded in his black and white scrawl.

Oh yes, he said, Now let me think, how many was it...

She didn't allow him the time to count: Do you think she did have tuberculosis? she said, Do you think she really did spend three years in the tower? Before eloping, I mean.

She heard the quiver in her voice and felt her insides shrink.

I wouldn't say so, no, he said. She wouldn't have survived into her eighties had that been the case. But, you see, he said, that's just my, *ah*, professional opinion.

She was grateful for his poise, for the gentle way in which he presented his version of things. And she wondered if there wasn't some sympathy between the work of the undertaker and the storyteller, both concerned with preservation and remembrance of lives past, both

156

dependent on colours and effects, on manipulation of the limbs and tricks of perception, to give the illusion of a warm body. To achieve the desired effect, they would do to their subject whatever was required; they closed mouths firmly with thread and wire, placed white discs on the eyeballs so they looked like two miniature full moons, then sealed the eyelids shut.

But let me tell you now, plainly, what T didn't know at the time: that the undertaker never would share with her all he knew, that after a couple more phone calls and a few more promises, that path, too, turned into a dead end.

.

Midnight came and went but she couldn't sleep. Her mind was unstill, she felt more awake than she had all day, though her limbs were like dead wood. She had started to develop a new cough which, before the undertaker's call, before those hours in the History Society storeroom, would have seemed to her freighted with eery coincidence. She would have milked it for all it was worth. Now, it was a nuisance, pure inconvenience, and a reminder of a magical way of thinking that no longer served her. She lay there in a duvet cloud, with one hand poking out to hold her phone to her face. She watched videos of A, running around hundreds of miles away, with a reindeer hat, short antlers nested between two pink crocheted ears. In another she played with blocks, blue, red and yellow. She had learnt to stack them one on top of the other, but while everyone encouraged her to build higher and higher, what A relished most was the moment the precarious tower toppled and broke against the floor. She gasped and clapped. 'More!'

She thought how much A looked like her at the same

age and remembered how, shortly after A was born, her sister had said: 'To see you holding her, it's like you've reached back through time and are holding yourself.'

¶ *I walked today for hours, almost four, and, as I dipped down to the river, I saw in the distance a grey bloated mass like old snow and knew immediately what had happened. A ewe had taken a tumble down the steep bank, broken her leg and drowned. I don't know if she struggled long or gave up the ghost as soon as she felt the icy shock of the water. The crows have had her eyes, they always do. I will tell Bessie later who will tell one of the groundsmen, and the body will be gone by morning. I gathered a handful of flowers, the last hawkbit of the year, the remnants of heather, brown and crisp, and cast it into the fast-flowing water. How thin is the line between life and death; one careless step and all is done, the decision made for you, irretrievably. And if you might just die tomorrow, should you not live each day as if it were your last, do as you feel and to hell with everyone else? I do think so, sometimes. But Patience is a girls' name; we get Constance from constancy, Irene from irenic. No one has ever named their daughter Courage or Will or Resilience. There is Liberty of course, but what sort of a trick is that?*

III.

At breakfast, everyone was exchanging news of the night's storm. Thousands of houses were without power, vast areas had flooded; people had fled their homes. People who had watched other people in faraway underwater places flee their homes, never thinking that one day the television crews would film *them*, fleeing their own.

You'll just have to hope you can get home tomorrow, the landlady said, as she set a neat row of triangular toast beside T's laptop. T smiled, said she could think of worse places to be stranded. The landlady smiled back, and as T watched her walk away, she imagined what would happen if she never went home, if events transpired to keep her there somehow, or something occurred along the way to prevent her safe return. She imagined her husband with his head in his hands, A saying *mamma* again and again, the wolf lying by the front door for a hundred years. She thought of the tragedy of a young family broken and started to feel her eyes prickle with salt.

She had always been able to do this, to create a surge of feeling in herself by picturing mawkish things, to move herself to tears. Actors could call it a skill. She thought of it as a way to pre-empt terrible things that might happen to her, such as being pierced through the heart by a rogue bullet during hunting season or crushed by a tree in high wind, so that, should one of these scenarios come to pass, she would at least have the dim satisfaction of having foreseen it, so that fate couldn't have the last laugh at her expense. This was in bed at night, usually, but she had fabulated on buses, planes, trains, while walking around the supermarket and on her way to collect A from nursery. A car mounting the pavement, a malign stranger, a collapsing bridge.

She was brought back to her triangular toast by music spitting intermittently from the speakers in the corner behind her, a jazz-piano froth, designed to fill time without making it in any way memorable. The same soundtrack had accompanied every meal she had had since arriving, lifting the bar-cum-dining room into a kind of present continuous moment. But the sadness stayed with her, laying itself over a sorrow with which she had woken. Until the revelations of the historian and the undertaker, Annie had for a decade or more occupied a space in her life, in her head and – if you'll allow – in her heart. She had felt for her, for the fact that she had suffered, and that nobody seemed to know or much care. Annie had been a never-ending source of feeling, a simple story in which injustice was unambiguous; no need to dig deep or examine anything too closely.

For the fact. In fact. The fact is. How many times had T said those words to add weight, to convince, to deflect? She would have to unpick so much now that maybe by the end nothing at all would be left of the story of Annie and her tower. And who, or what, would then come, unbidden, to take Annie's place?

.

She stood at the cemetery gates and checked the time on her phone as if she had somewhere else to be.

The sky was the colour of canned mushroom soup. The sun was pretending to fight its way through, but could not convince the rimy land. A muscular blue-black crow hopping along the path a little way ahead slapped his wings against the air and made for the trees. She had read somewhere that certain tribes believed the crow to be a guardian of human souls, that without his guiding

161

wing the dead became lost in an in-between, neither past nor present, an eternal there-not-there.

She followed the crow not to follow him, but because the group of trees whose dark canopy now concealed him also appeared on the map she held in the palm of her hand, an illuminated grid of numbers and names, whose computerized perfection seemed, unbelievably, to correspond to the reality through which she walked. The ground sagged in front of graves, the lawn undulating like cheap carpet. The map told her that as she reached the trees, she would find first, in a row, Charles Jnr, then Charles Snr, followed by Alice; and in a second, parallel row, directly behind Alice, lay their Annie.

But when she got there, she found nothing. She was under the trees, in a clearing between two giant holly bushes with dark glossy leaves and perfectly spherical berries like beads of fresh blood; she was exactly where she was supposed to be and yet there was nothing. The lawn was smooth, undisturbed. Tall graves stood all around, their names and dates in bold capital letters seeming to amplify the silence she had found among them. She walked back and forth for some time, covering not only the ground where Annie and her family were supposed to be, but also ground which, according to the map, was irrelevant to the search, just in case of some administrative error. It would not be the first time. She looked at the map and then at the lawn and then at the sky and felt that disappointed relief again. Then, she walked back towards the archway through which she had entered the cemetery. A man with a large shaggy dog passed her on the path and smiled, a warm, sorrowful side-smile.

He thinks I have lost someone dear to me, she thought, but I haven't lost her yet. Until I find her, I haven't lost her.

•

She had time to kill before the local authorities' offices opened again after lunch. When she had rung earlier, on her way back from the cemetery, a recorded message informed her that Bereavement Services was unavailable to take her call but that she should leave a message. She didn't because she was scared that if she were to explain what she was looking for and why it would come out all wrong; it would sound insane or illegal or at the very least inappropriate.

At the far end of town was a bookshop, the largest for miles, so she went to buy a book for A, as she did from most places she went without her, writing the place and date in the inside front cover. She wasn't entirely sure why she had started the tradition, had in fact given into the urge before coming up with a rationale to explain it. She wanted A to know she was always thinking of her, even when she wasn't with her, she said; or that she wanted her to grow up understanding that there were times and places other than her own. She wondered if there wasn't also a need to remind herself, while tidying A's room or reading her the same book for the thousandth time, that she had once been elsewhere, doing other things, and would be again one day.

She thought she might buy *The Magic Mountain*, too. She had a copy already, had it with her in fact, back at the inn, but she had got it into her head that it would be meaningful to have two copies to put side by side on the shelf at home: the first, which had been in her possession some twenty years, since university, when she read it and understood next to nothing; and the second, to commemorate this trip, when one of Mann's central messages, that time is what you make of it, had come into sharpest relief. Before, she thought, by which she meant before A, she would have found the observation empowering, a challenge rich in possibility; now, she could only feel it as a reproach. If she had failed to lay the foundations of a masterpiece in those three days away, she had simply not made the most of time and had only herself to blame. Perhaps Mann had not intended it that way, but that was how she took it. He had often said that the book should be read twice.

She turned a corner, and the bookshop appeared a little further along the road, and as she walked on, breathing clouds into the cold air, she thought how Mann's novel was also a study in how the individual could be reduced to the illness that afflicted them, to a series of involuntary symptoms and reactions. Although she thought 'reduced' was not the word, wondered if in fact it was the opposite. She pictured Hans clinging to an X-ray image of the tuberculous chest of his would-be lover, poring over patches of darkness and light; how he needed her to be sick, or everything would fall apart. She caught her reflection in the bookshop door as she pushed though.

The truth is, she had always intended to go to the bookshop that day. She had already pictured herself browsing the shelves, picking up a volume of Chekhov, perhaps, or something by Robert Louis Stevenson, Emily Brontë or Percy Bysshe Shelley. She had already written the scene into the screenplay of her time up there, in the village; between the shelves, she would reflect on the irony that, while being consumed by tuberculosis, these writers had dedicated themselves to their work in the fervent hope that it, and so they, might, in a sense, be consumed all over again, for all time. That the more ravaged by disease their bodies became, in fact, the more compulsively they created for the consumption of others, even while the effort

hastened their demise. In the end, Stevenson was confined to a shuttered room, his writing arm bound across
his chest.

Early in her research, she had read of how tuberculosis,
especially in its final stages, had become entwined with
obsessive artistic excellence in a myth of cause and effect;
she had noted down the words of one nineteenth-century
physician, knowing that he spoke for many when he said
that the disease brought a 'peculiar flow of spirits, and
uncommon quickness of genius'. The notion, although
resolutely debunked, had lingered in her mind. She had
nursed an image of Annie, alone in her prism, with pen
and paper, writing feverish lines no one would read,
whether because she didn't care to share them or because,
like her family home, they were destined to be lost, burnt
or torn to pieces. Some days T had allowed herself to
think that Annie too might have been a genius. There was
no proof to the contrary.

Because, she thought, even if you could hear Sontag's
warning and shake off hazy romance, there was grit in that
idea about time being what you made of it. Take Chekhov
and Mansfield, she thought: two spluttering wrecks, who
infused the short story with consciousness and complex-
ity never imagined in all the long, healthy lives before
them. Was it foolish, then, or vulgar, to suggest that the
peculiar intensity of their situations, the compression
of their very existence, might have shaped their art, that
their psyches whistled through every chosen word? She
thought of a line from the writer Natalia Ginzburg, that
'stylistic characteristics are always of an autobiographical
origin'. And so: what could Annie have done?

She took a breath. Perhaps more than anything, T had
wanted, in that bookshop, to explore the growing sense
in which, long after tuberculosis had laid waste to those

writers, she had herself taken on something of the appetite of the disease, devouring not so much the stories they had left behind as those others had told about them once they were no longer around to answer back. She had pursued them into the grave, she thought, and rigged their limbs to make them dance old dances as if they were new, partly because of a reluctance of hers to let go of that easy, compelling account of genius. Every time she had dismissed the theory, it seemed to pull her back again. Just because you know something isn't true, she thought, doesn't mean you stop believing it.

And maybe the fact that she could treat people that way, she thought, indulging in the tragedy of a short life, twisting the figures of history to suit her mood, suggested that she didn't feel as sincerely as she liked to think she did? Because there is also the matter of what time makes of you, she thought, how it softens this and hardens that. Had it been a question of an Annie dead the previous year, she thought, no doubt she would have felt and acted differently towards her; she would have been too close for such liberties. It took about a century, she figured, for a stranger to seem remote, unreal enough that we might treat them as we would a 'pure' creation of the mind. Maybe it happened quicker if they came from somewhere distant and unknown. She thought again of the undertaker's process, of how the veins were drained of blood, and formaldehyde injected to prevent decay and give the skin a lifelike plumpness. With time, it becomes more of an effort to connect with the dead, she thought, to feel for the historic subject as you would for the unknown woman you read about in your news feed just last week, who died after a long or short illness or in some freak accident. It can become more difficult to look at them and see yourself. Unless, of course, you have made some other connection.

But since it now seemed unlikely that Annie's lungs had ever been afflicted, the whole conceit fell apart before T had even reached the first shelf. She approached the desk instead and asked a man dressed in various shades of brown if he was the manager. He said he was, and so she said, Sorry, I'm wondering if, do you know, off the top of your head, which books sell best here? Would you have that kind of information?

He looked at her quizzically, so she explained that she was researching a book about storytelling, about why certain people were drawn to certain stories (for the nature of the thing had shifted slightly again, as if in a game of statues). She didn't mention Annie or the tower at all.

History, crime fiction and natural history, he said, pointing to each section around the shop. If you can write a book that covers all three, he said, you'll make a killing.

But has any one book sold particularly well in the past year? she asked, feeling like a cub reporter on her first story.

She expected him to name a crime thriller, so what came next was a surprise and a gift.

In the past two or so years, he said, with the look of someone who had been hoping for an opportunity to share his golden egg, we have sold 100 copies of George Orwell's *Why I Write*. Which is saying something, he said, for a shop with about 100,000 books to choose from.

Her incredulous smile was mirrored in his, as he lifted his palms to the sky and gave a small shake of the head. Disbelief is most delicious, she thought, when you know the thing to be true.

Why I Write was an unlikely bestseller. It was obligatory reading for English undergraduates, and she remembered it well, but there was no university for miles.

She suggested to the bookshop owner that it might be to do with the school, but he said he didn't think so: If we were talking about *Animal Farm* or *1984*, maybe, he said, brushing imaginary dust from the cover of a book beside him.

Written in 1946, Orwell's essay gave a clear-eyed account of the four main motives for writing that could, he thought, be found in different degrees in every writer. He wrote it, she recalled, just months after his first tubercular haemorrhage, which might account for the introspection, the shrewd eye turned on himself. (Four years later, he was dead.) The strength lay in its famous honesty, in lines she knew by heart such as 'Writing a book is a horrible, exhausting struggle, like a long bout of some painful illness,' that 'It is bound to be a failure, every book is a failure.' The motivations, which made writers feel more seen than they could bear, ranged from '(i) Sheer egoism', being a 'desire to seem clever, to be talked about, to be remembered after death, to get your own back on grown-ups' to '(iv) Political purpose', in which the word 'political' was to be understood 'in the widest possible sense': 'Desire to push the world in a certain direction, to alter other people's idea of the kind of society that they should strive after.'

And yet it was the third motivation, 'Historical impulse', by far the least raked over by Orwell, that had always intrigued T most: 'Desire to see things as they are, to find out true facts and store them up for the use of posterity.'

It had none of the punch of ego, she thought, less of the righteousness of politics. And yet: 'Desire to see things as they are,' those were not words that lay down to allow you to pass untroubled.

She remembered, too, the honesty of Orwell's gentle,

meandering introduction, in which he moved through his early years, confessing to decades in which he carried out 'a literary exercise of a quite different kind' to the important works for which he had, by then, become known. As a young boy, he said, he had begun to make up 'a continuous "story" about myself, a sort of diary existing only in the mind,' but in which 'I' became 'he'. At first, Orwell would picture himself 'as the hero of thrilling adventures', scripting his life as if it were a novel by Rider Haggard; but as he matured, his 'story' became less 'narcissistic in a crude way' (which is not to say less narcissistic overall) and developed in a more detached, descriptive vein, recounting in real-time what he did and saw. 'For minutes at a time,' he said,

> this kind of thing would be running through my head: "He pushed the door open and entered the room. A yellow beam of sunlight, filtering through the muslin curtains, slanted on to the table, where a matchbox, half-open, lay beside the inkpot. With his right hand in his pocket he moved across to the window. Down in the street a tortoiseshell cat was chasing a dead leaf," etc., etc.

The 'etc., etc.' had always got her, for some reason. The dismissiveness of it, but also its open-endedness. The story seemed to come 'almost against my will,' he said, 'under a kind of compulsion from outside'. He grew out of the habit, he said, coolly, although she wondered if he hadn't simply relegated it to a secret corner of himself, where it was that much easier to ignore.

.

Take a knife, he said. Or – with the curious conviction of one who had done it before – a tent peg. Just stick it in a few centimetres deep, he said, and, if you're in the right place, you'll hit something hard.

She was back at the cemetery, the words of the man in Bereavement Services playing over in her head. She had called again after the book shop, finally got through, and the man had given her new information: in 1909, Charles Snr had purchased a block of graves. Charles bought them not in the yard of the village church, but there, in then newly consecrated ground, on the fringes of society. The plot bordered his estate and, at that time of year, as T balled her hands in her pockets, when the trees' arms were bare and bony, she could see across to the hill where the manor once stood. The house was long gone, of course, but the tower lived on in its resurrected form, and on sunny days she imagined the light hitting the glass at an angle, making it flash bright as a beacon. But there were no such tricks today: the tower appeared to have been dissolved by rain into its surroundings, leaving little more than a faint white trace, like aspirin on the tongue.

The man from Bereavement Services had emailed another map, not so different from the first, and assured her that no gravestones had ever been removed (she had insinuated foul play).

Is it possible, she said, that Annie isn't buried there after all?

If she's here on this document, he said like a wise old sheriff who had seen it all, She's there in that ground.

He had sent photographs of some of the family gravestones, taken about ten years previously by the Records Office, part of a nationwide project to match paper burial records, such as those in the historian's colour-coded files, with real bodies in the ground. Alice and both

Charleses were present and correct. She pictured people up and down the land roaming cemeteries with their camera phones held aloft, bagging graves like Pokémon.

The grass must have grown over the grave since then, said the man from Bereavement Services. You'd never believe how fast it happens, he said, graves disappearing all the time so you'd never know they were there.

It was at that point that he had told her to dig.

(Am I allowed?, she said; It's only moss, he said.)

So now she paced around a small patch of grass, looking about for clues she knew weren't there, wondering where to begin. The science was inexact: the grid map gave her graves in other rows to use as markers from which to narrow down Annie's whereabouts, but the lines were distorted by trees, roots and bushes. Where Charles Snr should have been, for instance, was a large bush, a boxwood whose squared edges had long since rebelled against their sharp-fingered ruler. She plotted the invisible lines again, bringing them together like crosshairs on a space between the hollies, on exactly the spot where she had stood that morning, in the purplish shadow of a leylandii. Conifer needles in autumn's rust lay thick on the ground.

Clutching in her fist a teaspoon picked up from her room on her way back past the inn, she got down on one knee and made a first incision, stabbing the metal tip into the ground. Unbelievably – really, who could believe it? – she heard the high-pitched chip of stone. She adjusted her grip on the spoon, holding it like a pen now, and guided its edge back towards herself in a clean line, scraping stone all the way. Next, inserting the fingertips of both hands along the cut, she pulled the earth apart, peeling it back with ease, intact, so that it flopped open like an old paperback. She brushed a hand over the tablet, sweeping away loose soil, feeling the deep grooves of the engraving; the words were mostly caked in soil and illegible, although she knew already what they said. She fashioned a miniature broom out of twigs gathered nearby and dusted the surface of the stone like an archaeologist unearthing a tetradactyl wing, then stood back to admire the smooth, pale grey face of the stone: 'In Loving Memory of Elizabeth Annie', she read, 'who died on April 21st, 1977'.

Done.

She raised her hands over the grave, turned her phone to landscape mode, and took a photograph. She wasn't sure she would believe it otherwise, later, once all was out of sight and her imagination set about its work of interrogating and undermining the memory. She stood about for a little while, wiping her earthy hands on her jeans and reading the inscription over, wondering if the fact that Annie was mentioned as a daughter and as a widow but not as a mother meant that her line really had ended with her, albeit not at twenty-one in the tower. She wasn't sure it affected her one way or another – since the sudden elation of discovering the grave she felt, oddly, nothing – only it seemed clear that no one had visited that spot in a long time, if at all. Perhaps the undertaker, she thought, like the archivist, like the locals, like everyone, it seemed, who came into contact with Annie, had been misled by their own mind.

As she walked back to the inn, she wondered if she had done the right thing in leaving the earth parted, rather than closing it over again. What would the man with the shaggy dog think when he saw the freshly turned soil in the morning, through what dark turns might his imagination lead him? She stopped more than once and thought about going back. Was it worse to leave Annie exposed, only to be visited by nobody, or to cover her up again, as if no one had ever come to find her; to make her disappear again, so that the same old story could be told for another hundred years?

She knew she would never go back; knew she was done with Annie. Her story was left to tell – the elopement, the possibility of children, the reconciliation with her parents in the soil of her native parish – but T was not the one to tell it. She had felt this for some time already, had not needed the grave to confirm it. Annie was not what she had tried to make her: she had resisted in the end. T thought again of our cannibal nature; how Mansfield said we devoured each other all the time. How unctuous are the fats of another's life, how dizzying their sugars in our bloodstream, the infinite ways in which we may be altered, mutually. Stroking the cold, sharp edge of the teaspoon in her coat pocket, T asked herself in what sense she had hungered for Annie, what exactly she had desired in her but not received, or not enough to feel herself satisfied.

As she passed the church, she noticed the door slightly ajar so that yellow light spilled a little way into the night, turning the dull stone path to gold. She ought to go in and light a candle for Annie, she thought, in remembrance; it's just the sort of thing I'd ordinarily do. She pictured herself dropping a coin into the donation box, touching the waxed wick to one already aflame until it made that familiar, ancient fizzing sound, then gave way to a silky flicker, almost silent. But she couldn't go in. If she could no longer trust in the sincerity of her thought and actions, how could she expect anyone else to?

·

She headed one last time for the tower and because it was dark, rather than cut across the fields, she stuck to the main road. Occasionally a car came along and she was dazzled by headlights, and each time she wondered if this might be the driver who failed to see her dressed in black in the night. Every step felt unusually effortful and, by the time she reached the turning by the river, it seemed to have taken twice as long as the previous day. A pleasant kind of panic pulsed through her. I am the only reason I am here, she thought, rather than safe by the fire at the inn or at home reading A her bedtime book, that one about the train that ran away in search of excitement. She thought of Hans Castorp blinded by a snowstorm, how ten minutes seemed to him like twenty-four hours as he walked in ever more desperate circles, searching for some kind of sign from the heavens. But no path ahead called to him to follow and none behind promised to take him back the way he had come. Telesphorus was missing in action.

(She was in the field by now, where on the first day there were sheep; and they might have been there still, she thought, their fleeces saturated with night, silently listening to her boots in the mud and her heart knocking against her ribs.)

Nabokov had considered *The Magic Mountain* a waste of words. The novel was, he thought, devoid of beauty, while Mann's protagonist was little more than a puppet for his master's theories. '[H]e finds Mann's psychology and his characters made to develop so as to fit the author's teleological purpose,' Nabokov's wife Véra wrote to a professor, on her husband's behalf. Mann's prose was drenched in cliché. In another letter, which Nabokov condescended to write himself, he violently objected to seeing Mann listed alongside Proust and Joyce: 'What on earth is this pondering conventionalist, this tower of

174

triteness, doing between two sacred names?'

The things Nabokov most derided in *The Magic Mountain* were the qualities that attracted T. What Nabokov called cliché she thought of as a universal language of myths and dreams, an intimate register whose power lay in our innate fluency. A woman might have the eyes of a wolf, an apparently banal drink may alter you in unimaginable ways, time itself might slip its tracks and run away with you. She was drawn in by the novel as witness to the author's internal dialogue, where his ideas evolved from the rough and were tested in ever stranger arenas. How when Hans realized the ridiculousness of the idea that art and life existed in dichotomy, say, or understood that 'an interest in disease and death is only an expression of interest in life', it was really a dramatic reconstruction of Mann's own epiphanies, which, although they may have occurred decades earlier and in different circumstances, and been filtered through a different mind, were, on the page, revived and relived with the intensity of still unfurling situations. She liked that he collapsed the distinction between himself and his characters, that even now, a hundred years after the book's publication, she could watch him feel his way back to life through them.

Maybe, she thought, that was what Sontag had meant when she wrote, reflecting on a youthful obsession with Mann, that 'For me, he was a book,' not some mortal man who happened to live just up the road from her in Southern California. She had not yet had her own epiphany then, did not know that there was no 'up here' and 'down there'. When, in the late 1940s, she and a schoolfriend had gone to meet Mann, the encounter was dreamlike, between a 'fervid, literature-intoxicated child and a god in exile', between a frightened mouse and a

175

great, mythical moustachioed lion. A benevolent old lady (Mann's wife, Katia) magicked little cakes and poured rich tea from silver, while Mann spoke 'slowly, slowly', slower than seemed humanly possible. That Sontag could not remember how it all ended – 'how we were released' – only added to the unreality of the scene.

And yet it had happened, and Sontag's prevailing memory was of her own bone-crunching embarrassment. Before they went, she was, in anticipation, 'awash in shame and dread', thinking it 'grotesque that he should waste his time meeting me'. Her friend's idea – *she* would never have dared – was insane, 'ridiculous', pure folly. And yet Sontag went along with it. The reason she gave almost half a century later, an adult straining to reconnect with her childhood self, was that she had wanted to save her idol from the stupidity of the whole arrangement. 'As I revered Mann it was my duty to protect him,' she said.

But to T, Sontag, writing in some serious publication, was not being quite truthful. She was withholding something, failing to disclose a feeling, a ripple of the imagination, through fear perhaps that it would sound more ridiculous than the idea of two American high-schoolers sipping tea with a German master. If she had believed that she could mediate between Mann and her more foolish friend, then she must also have believed that some connection existed between herself and this living legend more than five times her age and with worlds and wars between them. She must, in other words, have divined, in that same embarrassed teenage body, an invisible thread running from her to him, some special unspoken sympathy. And what is that belief but a suspension of reason, a blind leap of faith?

T had had that once, not so long ago, a vague but unshakeable conviction that she and only she could touch a myth. For Sontag's ancient Mann she had had a young woman whom almost no one had heard of, and no one could trace, and that belief in a sympathy between them was the reason she was standing there in that moment, bones ground almost to dust, as, in nearest pitch black, she cupped her hands around her brow like the brim of a hood. She peered through the glass pane of a door into an octagonal room in which she knew no woman had ever lived. Still, she looked.

Stepping back a little to take a photograph by which to remember this epiphany of hers, how faith and folly were revealed to her as two sides of the same coin, she touched a thumb to the screen of her phone, and the flash, with a mind of its own, split the night. When she looked at the picture, ready to hit delete and take another, she saw her own reflection perfectly captured in the glass: a thin figure struck by lightning, her face nothing but a blaze.

She considered, then, how many times she had said *she* and *her* when really, she meant *I* and *me*, and pointed to other times and places, when really she was talking about her own; and how many others had said, or written, *she* and *her* or *he* and *him* or *they* and *them*, when really they meant *I* and *me*. If you could add them together, she thought, those unclaimed *I*s, stack them one on top of the other in a line, they would reach into space and scrape the surface of new planets. And if they were to speak all at once, the voice, if you could call it a voice, would be like the roar of all seas rushing land at once, ripping up houses, villages, forests, with uncompromising force, bringing awesome, unknown depths to bear. No tower of stone and glass could withstand such power. No tower of however many storeys would even stand a chance.

III.

A KIND OF FINDING

I

We don't always tell the story we want to tell. I said that at the beginning. We are each predisposed to certain stories, our thick or thin skins primed to be pricked, so that sometimes it may feel as if a story has chosen you; as if, rather than you telling it, it were telling you. There is a truth in every tale and your ability to see it – not just see, but rather to take and translate and carry it further down the line – determines whether you and a story make a match, whether you fit together like the pieces of a puzzle. And sometimes the truth may be especially well-hidden, like a pea beneath a hundred mattresses, sensed by some but not all, or not in the same way, a hard rub of recognition that leaves bruises in unspoken of places.

The impression is mutual. 'Every time a story is retold,' Walter Benjamin said, the process 'sinks the thing into the life of the storyteller, in order to bring it out of him again. Thus traces of the storyteller cling to the story the way the handprints of the potter cling to the clay vessel.'

But sometimes the truth catches the potter off guard. She might drop the vessel she is shaping, or pinch its walls too firmly, so that instead of leaving her print, she pierces the clay with her finger, puts a hole right in the middle, and is left wondering how she will ever bring it together again, if she even should. It will never hold water now. The story is not what she imagined, though; it's not a vessel, after all, or not that kind. It's a vessel like veins and capillaries are vessels, a vessel like the body. In her hands: a self-portrait.

II.

I was just shy of four years old when I had my first asthma attack. It is one of my earliest memories. Early summer, around midnight, a pair of arms reached out of the cool wall beside my bed and, with supernatural force, began to crush my chest so that each breath seemed to chase out the next and my heart was squeezed into my head. I cried for my mother to come from the room next door and told her there was a witch in the wall. At first, she didn't believe me. Then she did. I barely remember the rest.

From then, the witch visited every spring and summer, sometimes multiple times in quick succession. Other times, she sent evil toads to squat on my chest, their combined weight confining me to bed. That's how I remember it, at least. As I got older, it became less alarming, simply because I knew how it went.

There was a theory once that I had eaten bad mushrooms, so I avoided all mushrooms for some time; other theories centred on the neighbour's freshly cut lawn, the birch or chestnut trees, biological washing powder. A friend's kittens were blamed for licking me, and I am still nervous around cats, as if their saliva were pure poison. Blood tests soon followed, for which I would go into school late or leave early, with a note slipped to the teacher and the envy of my friends, and some of these involved a doctor drawing black tracks up my arms that looked like the crude stitching on Frankenstein's monster (I was proud, left my sleeves rolled up all day). Between the lines, a needle as fine as a silver hair pricked the skin and the doctor dropped something invisible and powerful onto each spot with a flick of the wrist and a whispered command, *graminaceae, felis catus, canis lupus...* Welts emerged like great pink lily pads, and the all-consuming itch was a lesson in how easy it might be to be driven mad, how you could lose your mind over the tiniest thing.

The state of my lungs came to occupy me and my parents near constantly. In the summer the air itself was a potential assailant; in the winter, a regular cold could turn to bronchitis or pneumonia with the conviction of a decision already made. I remember the faint whistle where my neck met my chest, which was an early warning sign; the soft beat of the doctor's fingers as they moved around my back, tapping, listening, tutting and sighing; the feeling of a cold stethoscope knocking against my shoulder blades. I breathed in and out slowly, my mouth open, coughed on command. I remember the word *rhonchi*.

There were hard white tablets to break into thirds and swallow with water, and yellow tablets to dissolve under the tongue but never suck or bite; there were sweet-smelling golden drops to swirl in water, fifteen morning and night; and tablets to crush with the flat of a spoon and mix with an odourless liquid in a little glass vessel with a delicate swan's neck. A stretchy tube connected the swan to an ugly machine, whose loud vibrations, like a thousand furious hornets, somehow turned the concoction to vapour, which was funnelled through a plastic mask towards my open mouth. The mask was too big, so my eyelashes and the whisps of hair that haloed my face glistened with dew; vapour became liquid again as soon as it touched skin, running down my cheeks like rain, dripping onto the table.

I had inhalers of every colour and shape, with extensions and secondary glass chambers that brayed like a harmonica if I breathed in too sharply. When I was about seven, I discovered that if I kept pumping the blue inhaler into my mouth until my tongue froze, the edges of my bedroom would disappear as a black tunnel spread from

the centre of my vision and dropped me into a mono-
chrome world of spinning, pulsating shapes. I heard the
throb of my heart in my ears, growing faster, and the
insistent *psst psst psst* of the compressed inhaler calling
me; everything else was distant echoes. I looked forward
to bedtime, to dipping under the duvet into the land of
black and white.

There were stays in hospital that seemed to last weeks
or months, but which I have since been told were only
days, five at most. I've seen the medical notes, and yet still
can't believe it, so different was my experience of those
days and nights, rigged up to a drip, discouraged from
leaving my bed or doing anything else that might exhaust
the little strength I had. I remember, one day, my teacher
appearing with a red folder full of drawings and paintings
from the children at school. In the pictures there were
dragons and lions and white horses and castles, and I was
always the princess with triangular skirts and a bright yellow crown. The walls of the children's ward that were my
home for however long it was were themselves painted
with vivid scenes from the books I'd grown up on, which
were the books we had all grown up on, children, parents
and doctors alike. A bright green beanstalk twisted along
the corridor, reaching towards the window at the far end,
to a world of giants and gold coins. There were thorns on
the beanstalk; I remember that, too, I think.

I remember wondering how it was that one minute I
was asleep in my bed or chasing my sister across a stage
where apparently some famous composer had once per-
formed, and the next I was here, propped up in a bed that
wasn't my own, beneath a semi-transparent tent, whose
magic air was supposedly making me better. I remember the sweat of what felt like an entire summer spent in
that hospital, in that oxygen tent, with the window open

onto blue sky, so that I could hear the bell of a school far below, and the noises of the children let out to play, the peals of laughter and the ringing-slap of a basketball on asphalt. I remember that I was up there, but not what I did for all those hours, whether I watched the small television suspended on an arm from the corner of the room or read books. I played cards with my mother, I think, and sometimes, if my oxygen levels permitted, I was allowed to follow the beanstalk to the playroom to choose a jigsaw or game.

I spent a lot of time daydreaming, eyes open or closed, about flight. I pictured myself in white pyjamas hovering above the bed and then sailing out of the window and down to the basketball court, where I perched on the hoop, like an exotic bird, to the amazed admiration of the children. Sometimes I had wings, other times, my arms alone. And though I say 'sailing' there was none of the easy grace that suggests: I had to expend a great deal of energy flapping my relatively small wings or lifting and lowering my arms in a pumping action, so that every centimetre of height was hard-won. The effort seemed to be the measure of believability; after one of these dreams, I swear I could feel the burn in the muscles of my back. It would never have crossed my mind to keep a diary of such things, because I was a child and nothing was happening in my life: no holidays, no daytrips, no parties. I didn't know about the inside world yet, didn't know that not every thought, desire or fear could or should be said out loud.

Mostly, I remember feeling weak, the doctors kept saying I was, but also special, different to the other children playing outside or painting me pictures. I knew something they didn't; how close to death we all are, that it was always just there, deciding whether to interrupt the day by throwing down its cloak of invisibility – ha! I've been here all along! – whether to reach out of the walls and suffocate you. For years after the attacks diminished in force and frequency, the last thing I did before falling asleep every night was to scoop out my hair and fan it across the pillow in a great swirl of chestnut; then, I would tuck the covers neatly under my elbows and bring my hands together, clasped gently one on top of the other over my chest. This was how I wished to be discovered should I die in the night, as peaceful as Sleeping Beauty, pricked by a thorn.

I haven't had an asthma attack in more than a decade; but still, every summer the smell of freshly cut grass introduces a note of anxiety to the day, and every winter, through chest infections that come with the predictability of a pendulum swing, I smell metal in the chill air and feel a cold knife press into my chest, its humbling tip on the breastbone, not as soft as Mansfield said. My lungs will probably be the end of me; I'll be weakened by old age, if I'm lucky, but I know that's how death will get in. And there is a strange kind of relief in that, in predicting the means of my own end.

If you have been ill, seriously ill, you will always be touched by it, always susceptible, if not to the disease itself, then to the ways of being and thinking it introduced, to moods and habits and preferences, to superstitions and other peculiar marriages of cause and effect. You will muddle on, swaddling yourself in all these things, telling yourself that the blade has grown duller, that it would take more to cut you down now than then, but you won't ever forget that the blade is there. And if you recover as I recovered, to luxuriate in the memory of illness as if it were a faraway land of snowy peaks and hot springs, you may find that you begin to pine for those long quiet days

186

in which you sat apart from the rest, high in the sky; when you dreamed during the day, creating other lives in your mind; when the structure of time was altered, so that rather than be carried in its steady flow, or dragged in its wake, you seemed to drop clean through it and sail away.

And yet, a curious thing: still now, just writing about my lungs, I begin to feel a familiar tightening, right here around the breastbone, like I can't take a breath deep enough, and a wheeze, like a knife grazing glass, escapes my lips.

III.

I told my publisher this book was about space, and when I started out, in a way, it was. Space and spaces. For what was Annie if not space, an absence of material, a mystery, uncolonized land? She wasn't a person; she was potential. And I couldn't resist. I claimed that space, worked it over, unravelled the mystery, diminished her potential. Then, I moved on. Or tried to, because I can't say I felt satisfied. The truth is I missed the emptiness; I missed the hunger.

·

When I was about ten, my parents started sending me and my sister every Wednesday after school to an elderly woman, who lived down the hill and gave lessons in watercolour painting. I used to look forward to going, partly because she had a fluffy dog you could pick up and cradle like a baby, partly because she was American and that is exciting when you're a non-American child, and partly because there was always lemonade in the kitchen, the extra-sugary sort that dries out your mouth and keeps you coming back for more. She had stacks of old travel magazines and encouraged us to choose a picture to copy as accurately as we could. My sister painted wild and colourful plants, indigenous people with difficult to render costumes and jewellery, elegant landscapes tinged by weather and season. I chose animals exclusively: a boxing hare; a badger standing, quizzically, by a fallen tree; a toucan curiously suspended although not in flight.

I remember her telling us not to fill in all the spaces in our compositions. 'Leave white!' 'Empty spaces, everyone, *empty spaces*!' 'White is light,' she said, 'white is *air*!' That she had to drill the idea into us gives a sense of how counterintuitive it was to that roomful of egos with loaded brushes. 'Don't fill it all in!'; it seemed, to me, an impossible instruction to follow. When I had finished my animal, I'd set about blocking in the background, painting in long grasses, rocks, trees, usually washing the sky in an unreal and cloudless cerulean blue. I stopped looking at the original photograph, stopped thinking about what the thing might actually look like. I remember the magnetism of the paint palette, the weight of the wet brush, the brightness of the idea to add just a little something else, there, to top it all off; the urge to declare the picture done. Done!

Horror vacui: a fear of empty spaces that leads the artist to supplement detail until every inch of negative space in the composition is transformed into something, a manifestation of some sort. I hadn't heard it named, my compulsion, until recently, when I was telling a friend about how uneasy I felt when I had dead time between things, a gap between, say, finishing the thing I was writing and collecting my daughter from nursery.

So I have to fill it with something, I said, I can't just sit with that little space, the emptiness of it, I have to Do Something with it...

Like horror vacui, she said.

Mm-hmm, I said, non-committal, so that she added: In art.

The conversation moved on; I moved it on, because I struggle to accept my own ignorance, experiencing each instance in which I don't know something I feel I should as a personal failure, a kind of humiliation. I make a mental note of those gaps – a concept in art, an historic political act, German words like *gesamtkunstwerk* – and later, I scrabble about, accruing fragments of information, references and quotations from authorities in the matter, so as never to find myself faced again with that particular blankness. There's a certain pleasure in this kind of knowledge acquisition, as embarrassment gives way to fragile enlightenment, a superficial sort of power that crackles and colours the edges of thought, like sugar under a blowtorch. But it's born of fear, a dread of exposure, of being caught not-knowing.

So, I added 'horror vacui' to my personal encyclopaedia, and read that the concept in art is grounded in an ancient understanding of physics, Aristotle having proposed that 'nature abhors an empty space', so that wherever there is a gap, things from all around will find their way into it. I pictured an empty house overrun with ivy and moss, where seeds blown in on the wind have sprouted between the floorboards. It wasn't specifically Annie's house I was thinking of.

Horror vacui was, I learnt, adapted by the twentieth-century Italian critic Mario Praz, who diagnosed it in Victorian art and design, where every perceivable space was busied with ornament. 'Diagnosed' because for Praz it was an undesirable condition, a kind of illness whose healthful opposite was an elegant modern form of minimalism. To fill the spaces is bad; the elements that do so are excessive, superfluous, the result of instinct rather than intellect, a subconscious tic that trumps the collected, higher self. The artist who fails to exercise restraint condemns the entire work.

Spaces! Leave empty spaces!

I wanted to, I did, but I couldn't. The urge to fill in the whiteness was greater. So, I washed paint into the spaces, as if to drown anything that might be waiting to reveal itself between my deliberate brushstrokes. Then I would start another picture, faithfully copying a monkey or a parrot from a magazine, mixing the colours carefully, touching my brush to the rough surface of the paper, repeating to myself a promise to allow the light in this time, to let the air move freely through the frame; to preserve the work from the breathlessness of autobiography.

It was the same with Annie, I think. I didn't know how to handle the white of her, the undefined and unknown that she was when I first encountered her – the uncertain name and date of birth, the completely unverifiable death, the everything in between. Those gaps in the picture of a life are lawless places and I tamed them the only way I knew how: I took up the brush and I filled them with the colours and textures I chose. I just didn't always know that I was choosing, let alone why.

IV.

When I try to understand what happened, I keep coming back to my grandfather, and how, in the advanced stages of his dementia, when his memory was more hole than whole, his stories became more vivid, more involving of him, and, by some measurements, less true.

A psychologist once explained it to me in terms of the brain, where memories are laid down in associative nodes, which interlink or run parallel to each other like the tightly packed grid system of lower Manhattan. Each node encapsulates a total experience. For instance: the sound of the wind in the bushes and distant traffic, the overwhelming smell of eucalyptus, the rich red of recently watered soil, the temperature and texture of someone's hand in yours, the joy of strolling through the park of a foreign city. There are, at any given time, she said, multiple routes to that memory, but diseases such as Alzheimer's create pothole after pothole until eventually there is no way back. What happens then is something like flight, a leap of faith guided by feeling, whether joy or fear or something else.

That *is* memory, she said, The thing you're trying to remember is the feeling, how it felt to be there in that moment.

An example: 'Grandad, tell me about the time you met Nana...' – a question designed to give him an easy time, to allow him to hold court how he used to. I thought, foolishly, it was a story he could never forget.

He began along a path I knew well, telling me about a dinner-dance near the Liverpool docks, about seeing her at a table with her sister and friends, how they didn't serve anything but tea at those places so he persuaded them all to go to a spot around the corner for a quick shandy and

192

a gin and lemon; how when they got back to the dance the guy on the door wouldn't let them in again. And just as I thought we were on the homestretch: pothole. The ground wasn't where it was supposed to be. At first, it may have felt to him as it did to me, as if he were falling; his feet running in the air, racing to the part where he walked her home, where they married and lived happily ever after. Meanwhile, the psychologist said, the brain – recognizing that, logically, the story needed an ending and his audience of one was waiting – reached for anything of substance and found something that had been there all along, automatic and absolutely true: the feeling of that night a lifetime ago.

It was the feeling, filtered through the prism of his life's passions, that made him fly. Suddenly, at the door to the dance, a fight broke out, a woman screamed, and two men threw each other about in the street. Grandad stepped in and punched one of them clean on the nose, so he, the villain, turned on his heel and ran. The other dusted himself off, and it was Frank Sinatra, exceedingly grateful of the help. So, the group was allowed back into the dance and Grandad was a hero; Sinatra joined the band to play a few slow dances for the new couple, and it really was, everyone agreed, an unbelievably magical night.

When there are gaps in the record – in a picture, in memory, in history – we fill them, compulsively, with imagination and feeling, with our own character, prejudices and desires, with infinite pieces of ourselves. We do it without knowing we are doing it, because we simply cannot tolerate the absence of colour or words, spoken or written in documents in neat black and white type. Or because we want to climb higher rather than fall in. Sometimes you will make a hero of yourself in the process; and sometimes this might be because, in another story, you were the one being punched on the nose or the faceless woman screaming.

V

I have been reading May Sinclair again. I bought the book the morning after I saw it displayed in the dark shop window. The man disentangled it from the fleecy spider's web and wrapped it in a piece of white tissue paper, like a shroud.

In one story, a man dies and goes to heaven, where he discovers that everyone lives in distinct universes, assembled from the fragments of each person's worldly knowledge and experience. Reality is circumscribed by the mind that creates it; their projection is the measure of them, like the old oak that couldn't grow much taller than the man who cut its branches.

Now, the new arrival must make his own universe.

'How?' he asks his celestial guide.

'By thinking of it. By wanting it. By imagining it.'

But as the imagination is under the dominion of memory, anything he brings to life in heaven will be a replica of something or someone he once knew on earth. No scenario will be truly original. Old fragments may add up differently, but that doesn't make the result new, exactly. Everything has already been written or said. There is not a thing that hasn't been seen before, not a feeling that hasn't been felt to a greater or lesser degree. Our man in heaven can only shuffle the cards, lay them out again, learn from them what he knows already somewhere inside himself, if he's honest.

VI.

Some memories you see through your own eyes, others, from the outside, from above, as if you were a director poised on a crane, making the movie of your life. Sometimes, in remembering a particular moment or scene, you might flit between the two, from the immediacy of immersion, the full-body experience, to the careful but slightly detached construction of a past reality, as if it were somebody else's; not *I* but *he* or *she*. Sometimes the process of othering yourself can tip into dissociation, when you fail to recognize the events as having involved you and so you do not integrate them into your sense of self. They used to say that only weak-minded people suffered from such disorders of the mind; they spoke of deficiencies, hysterical tendencies. Mostly, they spoke of women and people whose skin was not white.

More recently, psychologists conducting research into memory perspective have proposed three main reasons for a shift from the first to the third person:

1. You experienced unease or self-consciousness at the time the memory was laid down, perhaps because you were being observed. The brain is likely to recall the feeling and to try to imagine you as others saw you.

2. The memory is distant. In mid or late life, it's simply more difficult to put yourself back into the body and mind of the child you once were, to inhabit the moment in anything like a multi-dimensional way.

3. Trauma or an extreme emotion dominates. By switching to a third-person perspective, the brain

is trying to protect you – that's all the brain ever wants to do – to save you the pain of reliving the experience. One theory suggests that the feeling of remoteness reported by people who have narrowly escaped death, a sensation that their own end was playing out and they could only watch, generally from above, marks that moment of translation.

The three things can, of course, coexist; in fact, they tend to. They did for me – or is it 'do'?

.

If I didn't die that day, something inside me did, or else it thickened, toughened like a scar.

I was nine or ten – no one knows for sure because no one knew then that I would ask them to fill in the blanks decades later.

There was a smell of old chewing gum, when the mint has all but given way to stale saliva, and the strong coffee he must have had before, from a vending machine on the station platform. And washing powder, biological. I knew it by the way it hit the back of my throat as he pulled me up onto his lap. When his hand went up my top, my hearing went as if I'd suddenly plunged underwater. It's possible I've invented that detail.

Excuse me, she had said, my grandmother, as the train driver walked past our seats on his way to the cab. I wondered if you might show my granddaughter how you drive the train? She loves trains, she said. Or words to that effect.

Of course, he said. *Con piacere Signora*, with pleasure madame; once we're on the move, send her through to me.

It would be easy to say that I had had some presentiment, that some part of me had travelled ahead and knew what was to come, but I don't think it was the case. My reluctance to go was more to do with shyness, an extreme version that made it almost physically impossible for me to talk to strangers. It wasn't that I didn't trust them, I don't think, more that I was afraid of saying the wrong thing or of boring them; I could never think of what to say that they didn't probably already know.

When I knock on the door to his cab, I am myself, or close to it. I feel the hard laminated wood against my knuckles, and when I look over my shoulder, I see my grandmother at the far end of the carriage, smiling, egging me on. I look down and see the clothes I was wearing: a T-shirt with stripes in navy blue and orange, cargo jeans that were as baggy as my mother allowed but not as baggy as I would have liked, and the forest-green Vans that I adored. I must have been eleven, I realize now, because of those green shoes. Bought the previous summer on holiday, they were at least a size too big; I pulled the laces in like drawstring, so tight the suede ruched.

But as I step through the doorway and he turns around in his chair, beckoning me towards him, the perspective jumps. It happens every time, so that I'm looking down on us both now, this girl, small for her age, pretending to be a boy, and a cruel man pretending to be kind. Time seems to slow to let me take it all in. The light is dazzling, refracting through glass that wraps around three sides of the cabin, and things become abstract, so that I notice how a triangular side window has sliced the sun into a perfect replica triangle on the metal floor; and how the lines of his body as he swivels around, reaching an arm out to take hold of my shoulder, mirror those of my own, as I twist in the opposite direction, one arm crooked behind me, my fingers on the doorhandle, to close the door as he has told me to. I am young, everything about me is, I see that with the sharpness of a fresh razor. So, that point from the psychologists, that we switch to the third person in our memory in order to see ourselves as others saw us, it's like a punch to the stomach. Because, if I'm imagining myself from that man's perspective, all I can see is a confused and frightened child.

And then I'm back in my head, on his lap, chewing the peppermint gum he gave me, looking out of the window, speeding through green and grey spaces, fields and trees and houses and apartment blocks with people in their windows, daydreaming or doing the dishes; and I'm wondering if they can see me as I can see them, while his hands, warm, or not-cold, move over my back and my chest and my stomach – still a bit of a tummy, a child's pear-shaped tummy – and I sit there, mute, my feet dangling just above the floor. Part of me wonders if his searching hands weren't trying to discover the trick, that I wasn't really a girl; I had done such a good job of hiding the fact.

It was around this time, perhaps a little before, perhaps a little after, that I stopped writing in my diary. I definitely didn't write about what happened on the train; I wouldn't have had the language to express it. Instead, I took it into myself, sowed it like a seed deep in the soil of my belly and kept it in the dark thinking it would never grow. The adult me might explain the abandonment of that diary in terms of a shift in consciousness, might say something dramatic like 'the child died that day', or imagine a new 'I', Mansfield's 'new being', unready for the page, in denial of or in flight from the reality into which she had been pulled too soon. But I can't honestly say why I stopped writing the diary – ripped out its pages in fact, tore them into little squares and threw them away. Perhaps I felt I couldn't keep writing the stuff I used to, about birthday parties and holidays and the relative merits of different dog breeds, but knew that I wasn't equipped to write about much else. Perhaps I was afraid that someone, namely my parents, would find the diary and read it and that, somehow, I'd be in trouble. Or perhaps I had intuited how commonplace that incident on the train was, how little surprise it would hold for any reader, and how foolish of me not to have known from the very beginning how the story would go.

Sometimes, when my daughter is streaking around the living room before her bath, when I chase her and scoop her up and rub her convex belly, I'm surprised by a memory of that day on the train, by a flash of what it feels like to have a large, adult hand on your skin, how little it makes you feel. And when she giggles and says, 'More!' I think how far apart the two worlds are, mine and hers, then and now, that place of danger and this of absolute safety, and how powerless I am to keep it that way.

.

It was great, I said, I drove the train and a cow walked across the line, but I braked just in time to save her.

I remember that this seemed like the right thing to say to my grandmother when I returned to the seat opposite her by the window. A story that was believably unbelievable, that would paint me in a good light, as a bit of a hero, to impress her. Or maybe to distract her, or myself. It felt like the lines were already out of my mouth before she had even asked me if I had had a nice time, as if, just as soon as I stepped out of the cab, or maybe before, the idea had raced up my throat like an air bubble. Of course she knew it was a lie, only didn't know why, but she said nothing more, or nothing that I can remember now. Her hair was permed in those days, short and tight, silver washed with blue, and as she dipped her head to resume her crossword, I rested my eyes on the top of her head, trying to count each discrete curl. She must have thought I was staring past her, out of the window.

It was only a few years ago, when I first started to take myself back to that day, to will myself there, to – I don't know – try to piece together what happened in that bright light of a time and place when I should have been safe, that I wondered where that story about the cow on the tracks had come from, why it had arrived so easily, automatically. Just a few minutes on the internet solved the mystery of my subconscious: I had recreated a scene from an episode of *Thomas the Tank Engine*, my favourite childhood show, in which a heifer strays onto the tracks and all the engines fret about how best to move her on. (It was true what my grandmother said, I had always loved trains.) I found the episode online recently, watched it, and found that I remembered almost everything, except that the cow was clearly made of plastic and disproportionately small compared to the steam engines. And I had forgotten the detail of why she was on the tracks in the first place, if it had ever registered at all: that she was distraught because her calf had been taken from her that morning, sent to market on a train.

What would I have said had I not had that story on the tip of my tongue? I suppose I could have said less, said, 'It was great,' and left it at that, but I must have felt that a story of some sort was expected. It's funny, but in the moment, I think my instinct was to perform, to pull out fiction after fiction so as not to leave room for reality to set in, let alone to imagine what might have happened next had I not wriggled free (those thoughts came decades later). In fact, I staged an act as soon as I had fallen out of the driver's door, closing it tightly behind my back, when four or five teenage girls with their feet on the seats turned to look; their conversation stopped abruptly, and I remember wondering if they had been talking about me. I puffed out my chest and gave an exaggerated sigh, blowing air through my lips like a horse and shaking my head, as if to say, 'Well that was lame.' Or something. I don't know what reaction I was hoping for, but it wasn't laughter. The shock was shattering.

I see all this from above, too. I hear it and still feel a little of the explosive self-consciousness of then. They could only have been two or three years older than me. I've thought about them often, and wondered if any of them has ever remembered the tomboy with slightly too short trousers and goofy green shoes. And I've wondered if they might have known, or at least suspected, what had happened to me. Had it happened to them too? I've thought about the thinness of the wooden door to the cab, and how if one of them had just reached out a hand, without even standing up, she could have gripped the handle, opened the door, ended it in an instant. It's unrealistic, unfair, I know, but a part of me is angry with them for failing to play the role I needed of them, for leaving me, Little Red, without my huntsman.

VII

There is, I think, a natural sympathy between someone who has been seriously ill and someone who has
been abused. Both will feel a knife inside them, more or
less, forever. They will think about how much worse it
could have been, wonder whether they could have done
anything to prevent it, ask themselves whether what happened might have been, at least partly, down to their own
behaviour, somehow. Did they eat the mushroom they
were warned against, say the wrong thing at the wrong
time, go into a room they shouldn't have, place themselves
in the way of a danger they should have foreseen? They
will imagine and reimagine various scenarios, ones that
happened and ones that could have, and they'll feel sadness, anger and relief, but also fear that it might happen
again; if not to them then to someone they love, whom it
is their entire job to protect.

Above all, perhaps, you will never forget how powerless you were, and are, and how quickly someone's face
can change, how suddenly a fine day can turn bad. You'll
carry that knowledge until your last breath, and you will
not always know how, when or if, you should share it.
Because knowledge changes a person, alters their way
of being in the world, and you can never take it back.
I have seen it described, this kind of memory, as something in your blood, an antibody, a superpower. And
perhaps, sometimes, it is also an intoxicant, which can
cloud your vision and make you act in ways you otherwise wouldn't.

VIII.

I remember, I remember, I remember. Remember. Once you have said the word enough times it loses its meaning. More than seventy times in this book alone. How many in a lifetime? You forget that it means 'to call to mind' and find yourself dwelling instead on the word *member*. To re-member: to piece yourself back together from memories, as if from limbs and other body parts scattered by an explosion or foraging beasts.

But in that scenario, where bits of you are *I* and other bits *she*, where gaps are sometimes filled with whatever lies to hand, by whatever seems to fit the mood or the mould, isn't there a risk that you might inadvertently, mistakenly, remember yourself from the pieces of someone else, too? The same way as you might, in trying to rebuild a woman you never met, to bring her to life on the page a hundred years after her time, lend her parts of yourself or of other people you know or have only read about, without always realizing you have done so?

All because you have to tell a story, and it has to add up, has to grip; above all, it has to be believable, or at least believably unbelievable.

.

'How are we supposed to remember every single thing that happened and how it happened? We didn't write it down in a book.'

I was on the phone to a therapist who was explaining the main problem with the narrative imperative imposed on anyone who has been abused: the requirement that they tell us precisely what occurred, when and how. 'Because, people like to think, we *are* our memories

– like, they're the building blocks of our identity.' We like our stories to be linear, she said, with a logical sequence of cause and effect, one happening following the next, until the whole thing is laid out and gleamingly clear. 'But if you're talking about abuse or some other trauma you can't do that,' she said. 'You're in a fog, you're in a cloud, you're underwater.'

The thing that will hold you back time and again, so that sometimes you'll take your experience unspoken to the grave, is the fear of being met with disbelief, told that you made it all up. The accusation might be levelled by the person closest to you, by whom you wish to be believed, held, more than anyone. If I don't tell the story right, you think, this will happen, I'll be disbelieved, abandoned, ridiculed or reviled; one misstep, one detail out of place, and the whole thing will tumble down. The 'thing' being you. And you can't start again, not once they think you're a teller of tales. You may even start to wonder if you believe yourself.

We all know how it feels not to be taken at our word, the injustice of being accused of fibbing when we are not, the frustration and humiliation of being unable to give definitive proof. But not everyone knows how it feels not to be believed about something so intimate, so integral to your own understanding of who you are, where you have come from and where you might go next. Without that key, how can anyone understand why you can't do things they can, why certain places put you on edge, why you could never think the way they are asking you to think? And yet why risk doubt and suspicion when you could just bury the thing and push on? You've come this far, after all. Others have known worse and gone further.

So sometimes, often, in fact, you don't set out to share what happened to you at all. Sometimes, the therapist said, the choice is made for you, you're ambushed, ensnared by something that has nothing to do with you – by something in the news or that happened to someone you hardly know. A little light breaks through the crack, reaches the seed. 'And as soon as you start opening up, the flashbacks and nightmares begin.' She encourages people to write the nightmares down, to capture any thoughts that come to the surface. 'It will help you to find some kind of structure,' a door into what might seem like pure chaos or the first step in your unravelling. Writing it down can lend a sense of validity, she said; writing 'elevates' the experience.

It can also help, a writer told me many years ago, in a context unrelated to ours, to compose yourself in the third person, to build yourself at a remove; to create a little breathing space. We had been talking about writer's block, how sometimes words desert you and the only way to get them back is to trick them. I stored the idea until sometime in the second winter of the pandemic, when I had hardly thought about that day on the train for years. Or at least not overtly; an obscure part of me had probably been thinking about it all day every day since it happened. In the previous decade or so, I had told a few people, a carefully selected four, and never without anguish. But it seemed that hadn't been enough. I felt the urge to write it down, to get it published, to tell everyone but also no one. A short story about a girl on a train with her grandmother and a wolf in a navy-blue uniform; fiction, where belief was in a different currency. When I was finished, I read the story through, maybe twice, then waved my cursor over the pages and tapped delete. Then 'undo'. Delete again. I did this a few times to see how, or if, it made me feel, but if it did, I don't remember. Had I been expecting a cure? I never sent it to anyone to read, mostly because it wasn't good enough; it couldn't have told them anything they didn't already know about human nature.

I was pregnant at the time, about halfway along, far along enough to have named her, and too scared to go almost anywhere in case I got sick. I was convinced that, what with my weak chest – that innate vulnerability of mine – and an immune system compromised by pregnancy, it would be the end of me. And so, of her too. Lately, I have wondered if it was the fear of strangers and confined spaces that did it, that led me back to my eleven-year-old self. The dread of a threat that might come at any moment, and how, if it caught you, people might legitimately suggest that you had failed to take precautions and so were, at least partly, to blame. Were you wearing the latest recommended mask? *You* caught *it*, we say, not the other way around. Trains were again fraught spaces, high-risk environments.

I read about a study, around a decade old, in which the brains of mice were monitored for signs of memory suppression. The very idea was controversial, scientists being relatively confident then in their understanding of how memory worked: that pathways were established and followed in a logical fashion; that brain cells, or neurons, sent information along those well-travelled roads; that nothing could be concealed from the technology designed specifically to capture it. But suddenly there were subpaths, too, and these seemed only to manifest when a mouse was exposed to fear. According to the research, fear awakened a kind of cell receptor, for the $GABA_A$ amino acid, that could only be found in those subpaths. As a result, during fearful episodes, the mouse's brain appeared to bypass the expected memory pathways, opening new routes in the network, branching off on a diagonal, making oblique links. Less grid, more web.

There is still too much work to be done to say anything with certainty, but some people have suggested that the fear-memory response might become encoded in DNA and passed on to the next generation.

How strange to think that once your brain gets back to a memory, unlocked by the key of fear, it might find someone else playing out the experiences that shaped you, while you watch from above, noticing the light, the angles of bodies, the colour of shoes. Or not someone else, exactly, but rather another you, a *you* you no longer feel you are precisely because of that moment. You have been splintered by time and place and experience, like a mirror punched.

The question then is how to piece yourself back together again, to reconcile the perspectives, each an essential component of the *you* you are today: there's the person in the past, almost a stranger now, who was discovering life in real-time, unfiltered, and the person more identifiably you, looking back now with an eye for context and sequence, for narrative, with your cynical wisdom. And all the yous in between: the one who denied it, the one who thought she must have brought it on herself, the one who thought she should never tell a soul. I think you have to try, although I'm not entirely sure why. Something to do with owning your experience, making it yours again, rather than anybody else's. Moving on, perhaps, although that really just means releasing another you to the crowd. Therapists use words like 're-story', 're-author', as if it might all come off in the edit. Part of me believes this, too.

So, I have been reimagining what it means to be a person, what it means to say 'I'. Before, I thought 'I' was a tower, in which experience lay on top of experience, the weight of each unit compounding the other. A capital-T tower. The Tower was strong, could withstand all sorts of weather, but one sudden blow from the side might bring it down. Once toppled, the Tower could be rebuilt, but, even with the same stones, it would be substantially different to the 'I' of before; its mortar would be mixed of other stuff, new tools and fixes, crutches and staples, would have to be brought in to help it stand again. It would be, I guess, a pretty blatant and raggedy construction.

Now, though, I am thinking of a spider's orb-like web, of infinite fine interconnections. The web might be damaged by wind and rain, the swipe of a malicious hand, feisty prey, or an unexpected intruder, like a twig or a scrap of paper. The holes can be repaired, fresh lines thrown from one side to the other, like a sailor's ropes thrown to the shore. The web's original pattern is disrupted but the result is stronger, not weaker. I read that some spiders reel the silk strands in at the end of each day, unravelling their laborious creation bit by bit, ingesting the nourishing proteins, mixing them in the gut with the day's catch, in preparation to cast out a fresh web tomorrow, all made from the same stuff. A metaphor made manifest for what happens in our own sleeping brains. The spider will do this for as long as she lives, recycling, recombining, recasting, putting herself out there again and again because that's what survival looks like.

IX.

I am trying to own my experience.

After I have been on the phone to the therapist for some time, we begin to say our goodbyes. I promise to send her whatever I write about her so that she can check that I haven't misconstrued things, that I'm not painting the wrong picture or putting words in her mouth. I'm in a rush, as usual, to collect my daughter, so I have almost hung up when she says:

'Oh, um, hold on, I just want to ask: you know how everyone wants to share their story, right? I'm just wondering, what's the best way for *me* to do it?'

I tell her hastily about book proposals and agents and publishers and suggest that she go into a bookshop to browse the shelves where she'd like to imagine herself, to pull down the titles she most admires and see who published them. I tell her it probably won't be easy – she'll get rejections or, worse, no response at all – but there's every chance, if she writes a solid proposal, that someone will snap her up.

'And do I have to pay upfront,' she asks, 'or later?'

The question catches me off guard and for a moment I don't understand.

'You shouldn't have to pay someone to publish you,' I say. '*They* pay *you*.'

'Ah,' she says, 'because I've been approached twice where they say I have to pay them. I figured that's just how it works.'

When I pick up my daughter from nursery she is covered in paint and doesn't want to leave. The women running the place tell me she's always first and last at the activities table, that she's very expressive, always happy.

'Today,' one of them says, 'she has been saying her own

name non-stop, literally on loop.'

Her father and I have noticed this development ourselves. In the past few days, we have woken up to the sound of her calling for herself as if in a game of hide and seek. She says her name between mouthfuls of porridge at breakfast and in a steady stream as we chase her around the living room with her clothes. She says her name in surprised delight one moment, stabbing a perfect finger into her chest as if she has just discovered her own presence, and in indignation at being told what to do or not to do the next. It's as though her identity, her immediate circumstances and her emotions are all one and the same, a complete and indivisible self. She is, she is, she is.

I wonder at what point you start to doubt your own worth, to split yourself in two; into the part that thinks you are enough and should be heard unquestioningly, that anything you say might be interesting, and the other part, dominant, that can find lack in every limb and see logic in paying someone else to validate your story. My daughter doesn't know about the great economy of people yet, in which not all lives are created equal. She doesn't know how many poems through history have been signed 'Anon', doesn't know how many people have written under a name that wasn't their own, or paid to see their words in print, because it was the only way to be sure they would get any hearing at all. That they suffered for the privilege.

And so, she says her name over and over, reifying herself each time, thrilled to the tips of her toes. And occasionally she looks at me and jabs a finger and says *mamma mamma mamma*, just in case I am thinking of being someone else that day.

X.

Aloneness. That was a part of Annie's draw. When I pictured her in the tower on the hill she was always curled, like butter by a knife, over a book or a sheet of paper, melting into the words; everything she might need within easy reach, her world shrunk to arm's-length in all directions. A kind of self-sufficiency. She had few visitors, on account of being infectious; her days and nights were hers. The body trapped, the mind roaming. A fantastical aloneness, a vision steeped in the circumstances of my own life when I first met her, living in an apartment long since outgrown, in a building split with neighbours whose movements and voices I could hear at all hours, even when they were sleeping, in a city of some eight million people. Annie had what I wanted more than anything: space and time. It didn't seem to matter that she hadn't chosen them.

I guess I never craved an aloneness quite like Annie's, but her case took a longing I had always felt and turned up the heat, made it boil to see how much I could really handle. Her aloneness was the extreme tipping into perversion of an aloneness most of us have enjoyed and dreamt of having again: the untethered feeling of the sick but not too sick child, when daily life falls away, the expectations and obligations, the norms and routines, and we are in our bed in the middle of the day, hearing the world go on without us, feeling relief at being alive but not in life. We're just outside of things for the moment, drifting on a raft, with all the things we need: our books, the television remote, a plate of toast with butter, cool water; if we cannot stomach our dinner, we can have chocolate instead. There are kind people nearby, people we trust, who bring us these offerings, but we don't owe them anything. All they want is for us to get better; that is the only achievement that matters. Is there a freedom like it, once we are adults?

Virginia Woolf noted how being ill returns even the most mature among us to a child-like state, where your importance is elevated without your having wilfully or skilfully done anything to deserve it, where you are granted the undivided attention of those who care for you without having to pay it back. An allowed, even encouraged, self-centredness: *just you concentrate on getting better.* It's the perfect kind of aloneness, because you know you need only shout out when you have had enough, when aloneness turns into loneliness or fear, and someone will come running. Writing with the twin pains of tuberculosis and gonorrhoea, Katherine Mansfield poured hot scorn on her devoted carer Ida Baker – she was 'a curse', she said, 'like the curses in old tales' – but she knew that if Ida left, she would cease to be. Not that she would die, or not immediately; but she simply could not be alone without her.

After the early years of asthma attacks and mysterious allergic reactions, I spent a lot of time trying to rediscover some of the aloneness I had known. I even thought fondly of my sweaty oxygen tent, with its zip-up side panels and cloudy, crinkled plastic that blurred and distorted everything outside of it. I pulled a lot of sickies as a child. I would put my forehead on the radiator, go back to bed and call meekly for a parent to come and confirm how hot I was, that I would have to stay at home. I shattered a thermometer in a cup of tea once and in a panic pretended my shaky hands had dropped it; I could affect a wheeze until it became almost genuine. And then I would stay in bed reading books in which precocious children solved mysteries and/or passed into another realm just beyond the everyday to become wizards. I remember a collection of fairy tales in my father's study, Russian, I think, in which a young woman escaped to freedom on the back of a wolf. On its cover was a bird whose feathers were made of fire.

Time went by so slowly it was like it was made of different stuff to the time of forty-five-minute lessons and five-minute breaks in between. As I grew up, the sick days continued. Sometimes I took the duvet to the sofa and watched soaps in which everyone betrayed everyone, and crime procedurals, where women were found dead, often naked, and not brought to life in any way. Even then I felt an embarrassed kind of guilt, discerning in myself a weakness for sensation and gratuitous emotion. I always wanted to be made to cry.

Eventually, a letter from school put a stop to it. But by that point those drop-out days were too much a part of me to do without. I knew they were possible; they were my breathing space.

.

Space and time. When my daughter was born and I dived headfirst into a sea of love and devotion, the yearning was still there like a rip current. Sometimes it seemed to intensify in proportion to how impossible it seemed that I would ever again have either. There was a new guilt, too, so that if I now fantasized about flopping on the bed with a book or writing freely until my howling stomach or the encroaching darkness told me a full day had passed, I would then reproach myself sternly and worry that I was a bad mother moved by unnatural, selfish urges.

I wore her in a sling across my chest, because when I put her down, she cried, and soon I was wearing her all day and lying next to her all night, so she could hear me breathing, for sleepless hours that defied the hands on the clock ticking beside my head. If I could just find the time, I told myself, the aloneness, I could do something amazing; I could write a book or learn an instrument or start a business or volunteer or enter politics. But I had forgotten how to be alone, couldn't even navigate circumstances that might have created the opportunity. I refused generous offers to look after her for an hour so that I could sleep or work or do something 'for myself'. I put the words in scare quotes because they were a foreign concept to me: it was impossible, I said, because she fed constantly, and would never accept the bottle. She couldn't be without me.

Now I think it's not that I had forgotten how to be alone so much as that I'd come to dread it, to imagine that there would be some punishment for wanting what you shouldn't want, for taking more than you were lucky to have. And perhaps I thought that if I wasn't there for every minute, and if I didn't tell my husband precisely how to do what he already knew perfectly well how to do, there was a chance that the pair of them would realize they didn't need me after all, that I had done all I needed to by giving birth, and that now I could leave and, sure, they would be sad for a time, but really they could make do without me. My aloneness would then be redundancy, a pointlessness that cut to the core: if your baby doesn't need you, what are you? Are you still *mamma*?

It's difficult to say a few years down the line what I thought and felt in those early weeks and months of motherhood. I don't remember; people call it hormonal haze. In some respects, I think that woman wasn't me, I see her through a scuffed lens. But I do remember that one night I thought of a story I have known for as long as I can say, which goes like this:

Once upon a time, a woman looked out of her window and over the wall into the garden of her neighbour, a cruel ogress who, everyone knew, should never be crossed. The woman was pregnant and as she gazed from the window was overcome by a craving for the ogress's fragrant curly parsley. She longed for it until, one night, unable to resist, she sneaked into the garden and stole a handful. The next night she did the same and the next and the next until, on the fourth night, as she tugged a fistful of the herb, the ogress – who had been watching the whole time – revealed herself. 'Thief! Thief!' she cried, 'now you will pay the price for your greed.' Once the child was born, the ogress explained, the woman would have to hand it over. Either that or the ogress would kill her, or them, then and there.

When the woman gave birth to a daughter, with a full head of tight curls, she couldn't bear to part with her. She called her Prezzemolina, Little Parsley, and kept her close, telling her nothing of the world's danger. One day Prezzemolina, on a walk in the woods, encountered the ogress, who snatched her without explanation. From then, she was raised by that cruel stranger, who, jealous of Prezzemolina's beauty and wary lest anyone come to claim her, locked her in a tower on a hill, beyond the dark trees. There were no door and no stairs, so that the only way of gaining entry was by climbing Prezzemolina's long coiled hair, which she tumbled from the windows when the ogress commanded. The windows were high so that while she could see out, no one could see in.

Eventually – you know how it goes – a prince discovered the tower and the, by now, young woman and they fell in love at first sight. The prince visited regularly and said that when the moon had vanished, and they could be sure of the cover of darkness, he would bring a rope so they could escape. The town gossip got wind of the plan and mentioned it to the ogress, who only laughed: 'She won't get far without the three magic acorns I have hidden in the ceiling joists!' But the same way the word had got to the ogress, it now blew back to her prisoner, who found the acorns and waited for her prince.

The next moonless night, the couple descended from the tower and began to run through the wood. Immediately the ogress was on their heels, laughing and mocking them for dreaming of freedom. Prezzemolina turned and threw an acorn which, hitting the ground like a petard, transformed into a furious dog. The ogress, with a snort, threw a crust of bread from her pocket and continued with the chase. Prezzemolina dashed down a second acorn which, becoming a lion, hardly fared better: the ogress stripped the hide of a nearby donkey and, wearing it, charged at the lion, seeing it off. Prezzemolina, beginning to think that all was lost, hurled the final acorn. A wolf leapt from the shell and pounced on the ogress, still dressed as a donkey, devouring her from nose to tail.

The lovers were released from the curse and free to return to the prince's palace, where the king and queen gave them their blessings. They were married and lived happily ever after.

There was never any mention of the mother whose hunger for something that did not belong to her, for a taste she had no right to desire, wound up losing her the thing she wanted most. The thing she had grown inside herself, of her herself; her daughter, whose waxing presence had engendered those dreamy cravings in the first place. No, that woman is not even worthy of our pity.

I was thinking about the story again the other day, wondering why it was parsley of all things that the mother longed for, and of which she could never have enough.

In a dictionary of herbs, somewhere on the fringes of the internet, I found my reason: Parsley, the grass of the grateful. That woman fell for lack of gratitude.

XI.

Annie was the possibility of an untold and unowned story, a species that seems to be growing rarer every day but only because it had never really existed. There was so little proof that Annie had been one way or another, that she had been any way at all, so little to suggest there were descendants to claim her, that I felt free to make her mine. To a degree, others had already done this, so it wasn't as though I was crossing a line; I was only following their lead. And she would never know, anyway.

Later, after I had discovered the secret of Annie's long life – or it seemed a secret, so difficult was it to come by – I wondered how much, if anything, she had known about the stories to which she had given rise, whose tragic heroine she was. People told me that the story of Annie's death in the tower was being told in the 1950s and 1960s, while Annie was still alive, albeit not in her hometown anymore. Did word reach her wherever she had fled? Would it have amused or horrified her that people thought her dead? Or: did it give her wings?

Marie Bashkirtseff thought that fame was the only way to secure freedom – 'I shall be famous, I shall be great, or I shall die!', she wrote in her diary – because the more prominent you become, the higher you fly, the less people will be able to control you, the quieter will seem the critical voices. This would have been truer in her day, I suppose, before the advent of a circle of hell that could be held in the hand. But Bashkirtseff got her fame more than a century ago for that diary in which she documented every detail of herself, and yet still there is no freedom in sight, beyond the sorry kind death guarantees us all: the freedom of not being conscious of what others do to you.

So maybe, I thought, Annie's freedom was truer than

Bashkirtseff's because, as far as is known, Annie left us nothing of herself at all, no pieces to work with, no diaries, no paintings, no poems or books. She disappeared in life, eloped, dropping the obligations of her family and society like a heavy sack and running far away so that she didn't have to hear the terrible stories people told about her. I don't mean this naively; I know that wherever and with whomever she settled in the early decades of the twentieth century, she will still have been expected to conform to her role as a woman and a wife and, maybe, a mother, and that quite probably she wanted to.

The freedom I'm thinking of lies in the fact that, until recently, there were no documents to disprove the story people back home told about her time and again, that she was sickly and alone and dead by twenty-one. So that for all the years that followed – from the last census record on which she could be found by the old name, in 1911, to what transpired as her actual death, under a new name, in 1977 – while they were absorbed in that story, she was living in open waters, beyond their reach (and, perhaps, beyond their interest, for they already had the tale that satisfied them). Maybe, then, the story about the young woman who died in the tower is a kind of mistranslation of events whose essence is true: one Annie did die young, and another Annie was born; a woman who escaped attention and whose life remained her own to tell. She chose not to.

And yet, as much as I might stiffen at Bashkirtseff's bold revelations and savour the notion of a life less visible, here I am making my own marks, leaving traces, exposing myself to the public like Blanche Monnier, asking to be seen. Fearing the criticism that will come and my own powerlessness to influence or stop it.

She knew what she was doing.

She did it to herself.

I have been thinking about the word 'own'. This morning, I wrote it down on the back of an electricity bill, alongside 'to own it', in which construction 'it' is life, the self and everything that makes or threatens to unmake it. To put it down on the page, to make art out of it; to create out of damage and near destruction. If you own your self, I wonder, are you bound to sell it, provided the method and means? (Is telling selling?) Is there some ineluctable impulse, a reversion to the *I am I am I am* of the early years? Something like Orwell's 'sheer egoism', the first of his four great motives for writing, being a 'desire to seem clever, to be talked about, to be remembered after death, to get your own back on grown-ups' – but sharper. If you are not compelled like Bashkirtseff, and perhaps Mansfield too, by some gamble on freedom through fame, might you instead, given half the chance, sell your self because of a fear – irrational, perhaps instinctual – that if you don't, someone else might reach back to you from the future and do it for you, in parts or whole, renamed and reframed to their own taste, in matte or satin finish, at a price you have not agreed? And so, in the end, it is always you who pays.

XII

It rankles me that he knew what was going to happen to me before I did, as if he was ahead in the future, my future, looking back at me, sitting around in the past, beside my grandmother on the train, swinging my legs from the seat, all ignorance and innocence. Afterwards, it wasn't so much betrayal that I felt – for that, my trust in him would have had to be more conscious than it was – but humiliation, a feeling of foolishness, like I should have known what he knew, shouldn't have been tricked into entering his lair. Perhaps this is projection, a casting back to then what I know about the world now. But, afterwards, if ever my brain mapped its way back to that day, the first thing it encountered was a feeling of embarrassment at having been caught unawares, of having been *done to*; then the sound of teenage laughter.

The anger came more recently, a futile kind of frenzy, like cold fire. It still surprises me sometimes, that silver fury, flashing up when I am not expecting it, looking for routes to expression I have denied it, finding its likeness in odd places and seeking to impose itself; to connect with me in the present. Like one day, for instance, when I was thinking about Ariadne, how she believed Theseus to be in love with her, only to wake one morning and find that he had tossed her aside like an old receipt.

I had been reading Bashkirtseff's diary again, where, in 1882, she wrote of a sketch of Ariadne, three years in the planning, which she dreamed of translating into marble. She captured the moment of Ariadne's betrayal, the moment that came to define her:

Theseus has fled during the night. Ariadne, finding herself alone at daybreak, runs all over the island in every direction, when with the first ray of the sun, as she has reached the point of a rock, she sees the vessel, like a point on the horizon.... Then.... *That* is the moment to seize and difficult to describe; she can get no farther, she cannot call; water is all round her, and the vessel is only a point which is scarcely visible; then she falls on the rock with her head on her right arm in a position which should express all the horror of the desertion, of the despair of that woman left there in such a cowardly manner....

Water is all around; there is nowhere to go, no one to appeal to. Ariadne has fallen to the ground, and yet she is not drained, but full. There is, Bashkirtseff says, 'an utter dejection to be expressed which takes powerful hold of me. You understand, she is *there* at the extreme point of the rock, exhausted with grief and, in my opinion, with impotent rage; there is an entire abandonment, the end of everything!'

Imagining Bashkirtseff's unmade sculpture, my mind said that what Ariadne felt was humiliation. *Humilis*, Latin for 'on the ground', as low as you can go while still breathing. Mortification: part of her, dead. The realization that this man whom she had trusted had known her fate before she did, that he had played his hand in it. Ariadne's grief was not so much for a person as for an old way of thinking, for a warm blanket of belief, a favourite story in which the good prevailed, which she had told herself at the end of every day but could no longer; for a whole way of being in the world. The end of everything, then.

It wasn't cold stone I pictured, though, it was still-living flesh folded on itself, the head on the right arm, muscles juddering to sustain the pose, her face turned to the horizon painted on a silk screen: Bashkirtseff in the photographer's studio, wrapped around in a white sheet ample enough to rival the sail of Theseus's vanishing ship. She may never have taken Ariadne's name, as Mansfield did, but how could she not have seen, or felt, in Ariadne's awakening a rehearsal of her own moment: the dawning understanding that, for all her plans to be free, the fates had always known she would end up alone on a rock, surrounded by the ocean and the memories of a more innocent, ignorant time? Perhaps that was the truth that had caught her eye, the mirror glinting, the story whispering to be told.

XIII.

I must tell you that I wasn't alone at the oak tree that day.
I said I was, but I wasn't. A friend, the one I said I spoke
to on the phone, who explained the peculiar appearance
of the tree, she was with me. She told me all she knew
about the tree hay and the deep roots in person. I didn't
mention it earlier because it would have changed the way
you pictured the scene, the way you held me in relation to
everything else. It would have broken the spell – wouldn't
it? – if I had told you that before we set off to find the tree,
we went for pumpkin soup and laughed at the obscene
amount of butter I put on my bread, that all the while we
walked up towards the ruins of the old house in the rain,
we talked of nothing but ourselves and our daughters,
that Annie wasn't on my mind at all for those hours we
spent together.

This is just one of the things I could have told you but
didn't. Like the locked-unlocked doors of the mother-
and-baby home, I played a trick – a little of Henry Peach
Robinson's 'interference', more elision than lie, in my
case – in the name of story. Because I must have some
control over the material, and so, I suppose, over you.
That's what you came here for.

Will you now distrust everything I have told you?

XIV

My daughter has a wooden trainset and she loves to push the brightly painted carriages around, looping back and forth in a figure-eight, under and over the bridge, pressing the wheels into the beech wood ruts, so that with every return, it becomes a shade more difficult, imperceptibly but irreversibly, for the train to come loose, to deviate from the track. A figure-eight, like the symbol of infinity. I wonder if she is old enough yet to imagine herself inside one of the carriages.

We tell our children stories so that they might see themselves in the characters, something of their own lives in fantastic scenarios, with just the right amount of threat, a lesson to carry into their own world. They like nothing more than repetition: there is safety in it; no surprises, no twists to jeopardize the ending they long for. Perhaps their mind is always already at the end, waiting for you, adult, turning the pages, to catch up. By the second telling they know all is not lost when the wolf licks his lips, that the huntsman will come. That the princess won't remain in the cold tower long. When do you tell them that in life there is no such neatness, no such guarantee?

When I first started going back to that day on the train – deliberately, I mean, with an adult's will to confront – I thought that by remembering I would work things through, process the experience I couldn't as a child, and so, be rid of it, free myself from the grip of the past. I believed in catharsis. That day so long ago would come to impress less on my life, I thought, but the opposite seems to be true. The more visible the memory has become, the more words I have written to exorcize it, the more difficult I find it to recognize myself in the frame. I am the me of the past again, in a sense, the me of that very moment, under the influence of someone else, objectified, man-handled into place. I have been trying to fix things again, to whip up a miracle cream to vanish misfortune.

Lately I have been wondering if I will ever tell my daughter the story of what happened to me or if, like Prezzemolina's mother, I'll keep the truth of the world from her, hoping for the best, fearing the worst. It would not be like me to encourage such unruly spaces, such places of unpreparedness. So, when will she be old enough to understand, for instance, that strangers must earn our trust (and may never manage), that you are not to blame for what others do to you, that one man is not all men? Show me the story that will explain to her why I don't think I will ever be able to let her out of my sight (and yes I know all parents believe this). Isn't it my job to give her those first lessons in what it is to be a girl? Would I tell her that it happened to me, or would I say that some-one else went into the driver's cabin that day, that she was called Prezzemolina or Rapunzel or Little Red Riding Hood or T? Could I tell it in such a way that the man himself disappears, so that he doesn't figure in our lives any more than is strictly necessary, for narrative logic? She would not recognize the threat of a wolf because she has a wolf for a brother, who licks her feet every morning before breakfast and every night before her bath. Her language is already different that way.

Recently, sorting through my grandmother's attic, we found a store of the books my sister and I grew up on, large hardback collections with watercolour princesses and princes, ivy-wrapped stone towers and fearsome wolves with long red tongues and sharp fangs like scythes. I took them home with me, excited at the prospect of making my past converge with my daughter's present. But when I unpacked the box, I stood there holding the books for a while, staring into space, not really thinking anything that I can remember. Then I hid them.

XV.

When I texted my husband to tell him what I had found, that Annie hadn't died in the tower in 1911 and had apparently lived well into the 1970s, his response – 'That's great!' – perplexed me, as if we were speaking different languages. The three dots forming and reforming on his screen 200 miles away, as I typed and retyped my reply, must have told him things were not so clear-cut for me. Probably he knew it already.

We hunger for stories that confirm what we already think or feel to be true, even if what we think or feel to be true causes us or others pain. The thing about abuse is that it limits the roles you see for yourself and others and reduces plot variation, so the loops of repetition become ever tighter, each constricting like so many nooses around life's potential. Ariadne will fall to her knees time after time because you simply cannot imagine a world in which she stands up proud, shakes her fist at the sky and sets about finding her way off the rock. It's both a frustration and a relief, to be honest, because it's easier to tell a story you already know than it is to let go of the familiar and reach for a reality so complex that no one has found the tale to contain it.

You don't want to tell your story, the therapist said, But it's the only one you've got, and you need it to be true because otherwise you have to reassess everything you think you are and everything you think you know about how the world works.

It's difficult to recast yourself, she said, Especially later in life.

'Your story' is my story, the story of what happened that made me see things as I have tended to. But the therapist's words spoke just as clearly to the other stories I

230

might take into myself: the ones that catch my eye in the news cycle so that I tell them to a friend over lunch; the ones I click through to during an idle half-hour on a train platform; the ones I write down for people I don't know to read. I'm thinking of Annie again, of how when I discovered that her life had not ended tragically, I struggled to stay connected, to remain invested. I doubted the truth of the revelation for as long as I could – I used words like 'it seems' and 'apparently', to undermine and unsettle – and then felt something like grief when I realized I could doubt it no more. The escape from the tower, the elopement, a presumed happy ending – it didn't resonate as deeply as my tale of persecution, in which the tower remained locked, as it is today. To tell Annie's story the new way would have been like trying to reshape baked clay.

It's not easy to let go of a story that means something to you and by which, in some warped way, you understand yourself. I think, in fact, it might be impossible, that you are destined to hold it inside you forever, to feel it digging into your insides whenever you encounter something that chimes somehow. It will press into your throat and ask to be told again. You may resist it, but it's there, however deeply you have buried it. Some truth must be in it for you, still.

Sometimes, you are so bent on expressing that truth that you have carried for so long, that you fulfil its prophecy yourself. We have all heard of the cycle of violence, how the abused can become the abuser. How else should I understand the way I took Annie's life and twisted it? The way I saw what was possible for her and denied it? The way her pain gave me pleasure in its telling?

I did try to find her family, you know, any great-grandchildren or nieces or nephews or cousins who might still be living. I wanted to ask them if they remembered Annie and what she was like. Was she happy? Was she healthy? What kind of existence was hers? And did they know that she was buried back in the family plot beside her parents, where the grass had healed over as if she had never been there at all? That I had found her for them, pulled back the turf with my bare hands. I thought I would tell them the story of the young woman in the tower first, without relating it to Annie and ask them if they had ever heard it before. I imagined countless conversations, but when I tracked down a family tree posted online – compiled, I figured, by one such relative – and clicked the button to contact the tree's owner, I received no response. I tried once more and then never again. I suppose I can't really have wanted to find them that much.

I have been thinking about Mansfield again, about a letter she wrote to a friend. 'I am so sick of all this modern seeking which ends in seeking,' she said. 'Seek by all means, but the text goes on that ye shall find. And although, of course, there can be no ultimate finding, there is a kind of finding by the way which is enough, is sufficient.'

I'm not sure what I have found along the way; I doubt I have told you anything you didn't already know. That the mind plays tricks, that truth is a broken mirror and trust as beautiful as it is breakable. That ogres exist everywhere, in everyone, so they aren't really ogres after all, just people. I have found that we don't always want to find, that we might believe or pretend that we do, while we try instead to hide things from ourselves, so that we can keep telling the same old story the same old way, never having to question our place in it or how it will end.

It's been weighing on me, the end. How to do it, I mean. I don't seem to have any of the required components.

I think this is partly why I have been reluctant to call the archivist; I've put it off for months now. I could have told her that I found Annie the very day I had, when I unexpectedly saw her that evening at the inn with friends. My miniature silver shovel was still in my pocket as I told her in vaguest terms what I had been doing since we sat together in the tower, 'trying to figure out what happened'.

She had never believed the story about Annie. She had told me this in a casual way when we first met on the hill and had appeared puzzled by my – I suppose, hesitant – tone when discussing the tower and Annie and what was said about the place. So, it's not that I'm worried about dispelling any illusion of hers, of making her feel a fool with my great revelation. She has built nothing on these grounds, as far as I know she has nothing at stake.

The reticence comes, I think, from the realization that the story is over, and it is definitely and irretrievably not the story I thought I was telling. But there is also a possessiveness at play: I wanted to keep the knowledge to myself, to be the only person who knew for sure where and when Annie came to rest. I can't explain the reasoning, except that the behaviour felt somehow instinctive, like a dog with a chalk-white bone, imagining the flavour back to freshness.

I have been telling myself stories again. The other night I remembered the photograph of the writer-not-historian, with the 1950s pin curls and summer dress, posing with her friend in front of the tower, some years before it fell into disrepair. The historian and I did not discuss the identity of the second woman; to be honest, I had forgotten all about her until that moment, sometime between midnight and two in the morning.

Now, though, when I need her to satisfy some impulse

233

in me, I summon her, imagining that she is Annie, back to visit the land of her past, where the house no longer stands but memories hang in the trees like her mother's Chypre. I picture her walking through the village, on market day, taking in the changes; her father's old shop no longer there, a bus stop where the horses used to rest. And if she were to stop someone at random in the street to ask them whether they knew what happened to the family that once lived on the hill, what would they tell her? About the extravagant wealth and the fur coats, how it all vanished overnight, about the fire, and the tragedy of the girl in the tower?

I make it happen. The stranger – a composite of several men I met, with yellow eyes and smiling faces – is affable enough. Sharing one story and then another, as if none of the people involved was ever real. He points her in the direction of the writer's home, at the bottom of the dead end called The Folly, where the famous knitting woman once tapped time with her needles: Go and see her if you want to know more, he says, never suspecting that this offcomer knows everything already, that she is playing a kind of game with her own life. I imagine Annie appearing on the writer's doorstep to say, Look! I am alive and well, that her only real complaint is a little arthritis in the right wrist.

It is a glorious day in my story, the kind that warms every fibre of you, and so one of the women suggests a walk up to the tower, to dot the *i* and cross the *t* of the story once and for all, with a photograph. Because you can't say truer than a photograph. A third person must have been with them, then, to take it. And here, the story runs out of ground. I feel the earth give way beneath me and a rush of air; I pull back, tired from trying to make everything fit.

When I do eventually telephone the archivist, I tell

her what I have discovered. That both Charles Jnr and Annie lived into old age, that there was no fire, that tuberculosis was very unlikely all things considered, and that there may have been an elopement, perhaps children too. I say that Annie had been there all along, by the way, in the cemetery we could see as we talked in the tower, that I had dug her up, quite literally, and left the earth parted, 'should you wish to visit her'.

And I tell her about my new theory, that the anonymous woman in the photograph with the writer might just be Annie.

It's possible, I say. I mean, does anyone know who that other woman is?

The archivist, as helpful as ever, says she knows someone who might be able to fill in the gaps of my research, that she'll email her contact right away to ask. She mentions a community forum that might have more answers, that we might be able to trace the children of the children.

I make all the right noises – enthusiastic, earnest – but really, I have almost stopped listening to what the archivist is saying. I never doubted that I could find out who the woman was, if only I wanted to.

Some Notes and Citations

13   *'a story about a woman who became trapped in a suffocating vision of the afterlife'*: The story is May Sinclair's 'Where their Fire is not Quenched', in *Uncanny Stories* (London: Macmillan, 1923). The story referred to on p.195 is 'The Finding of the Absolute', in the same collection.

24   *'The lifestyle of the family'*: Joyce Scobie, 'Akay: The Story of an Estate', courtesy of Sedbergh History Society.

27   *'Without a doubt there exist'*: The words of Gustave Le Bon (1841–1931), quoted in Stephen J. Gould, *The Panda's Thumb: More Reflections in Natural History* (New York: W. W. Norton & Company, 1980).

28   *'only in part for their pedagogical value; they were used'*: Carol Dyhouse, *Growing up in Late Victorian and Edwardian England* (London: Routledge, 1981).

28   *'open children's letters, superintend their reading'* and *'became almost obligatory companions'*: Peter Gay, *The Bourgeois Experience, Victoria to Freud: Education of the Senses, Volume 1* (Oxford: Oxford University Press, 1985).

29   *'Almost all diaries contain at least one moment'*: J. H. Hunter, 'Inscribing the Self in the Heart of the Family: Diaries and Girlhood in Late-Victorian America', *American Quarterly*, volume 44, issue 1 (1992).

29   *'Nothing has happened until it has been described'*: Virginia Woolf, as spoken to her biographer Nigel Nicolson, *Virginia Woolf* (London: Viking, 2000).

36   Susan Sontag, *Illness as Metaphor* (New York: Farrar, Straus and Giroux, 1978).

36   Much of the medical history in these pages and beyond is drawn from Thomas Dormandy, *The White Death: A History of Tuberculosis* (London: Hambledon Continuum, 1998).

37   *'shy, evasive, glassy-eyed manner of speech'*: Franz Kafka, in a letter from April 1924, quoted by Sontag.

37   *'leaden-eyed despairs ... spectre-thin, and dies'*: John Keats, 'Ode to a Nightingale' (1819).

40   The film can be found in two parts in the archive of the Wellcome
     Collection: 'Collapse therapy in the treatment of pulmonary
     tuberculosis' (Chicago, *c.* 1925), Reel one: https://wellcomecollection.
     org/works/sbvzms7t
     Reel two: https://wellcomecollection.org/works/ba6nkw3q

46   '*Emmeline says she will send me* The Blue Lagoon, *just as soon as she has
     finished reading it herself*': Henry De Vere Stacpoole, *The Blue Lagoon*
     (London: T. Fisher Unwin, 1908).

47   All sources mentioned in chapter VI – posters, advertisements, etc. –
     can be found in the archives of the Wellcome Collection.

48   References to the work of John Davy Rolleston draw on two related
     articles: 'The Folk-Lore of Pulmonary Tuberculosis' (March 1941) and
     'Respiratory Folk-Lore' (January–February 1944), both published in
     Tubercule.

51   Anna Jackson's paper is 'The "Notebooks", "Journal", and Papers of
     Katherine Mansfield: Is Any of This Her Diary?', published in the
     Journal of New Zealand Literature, No. 18/19 (2000/2001).

57   For chapter VII, I consulted, among other sources, an article by Sonia
     Wilson, '"I Am My Own Heroine": How Marie Bashkirtseff Rewrote
     the Route to Fame', published by Public Domain: publicdomainreview.
     org/essay/marie-bashkirtseff/

78   Quotations from Carl Jung are from *Memories, Dreams, Reflections: An
     Autobiography*, translated by Richard and Clara Winston (London:
     Collins and Routledge & Kegan Paul, 1963).

90   The review of *The Book of Wonderful Characters* is by Miranda France,
     'Telling details: On attempts to capture people in words' (London: *The
     Times Literary Supplement*, 1 September 2023).

91   Walter Benjamin's essay is 'The Storyteller' (1936), included in
     Illuminations, translated by Harry Zohn (New York: Schocken Books,
     1969).

95   Claire Tomalin, *Katherine Mansfield: A Secret Life* (London: Viking,
     1987).

152 The strange stories (the Bird Man, the Faire Hunter, etc.) are drawn
     from the work of the late '*writer-not-historian*' Freda Trott, *These We
     Have Known* (UK: T. W. Douglas & Son, 2001).

165 *'peculiar flow of spirits, and uncommon quickness of genius'*: These are the words of the physician Andrew Duncan (1744–1828).

174 My reference to *'the train that ran away in search of excitement'* is to Graham Greene, *The Little Train*, illustrated by Edward Ardizzone (London: Bodley Head, 1973).

175 Susan Sontag's account of meeting Thomas Mann was published as 'Pilgrimage', in the *New Yorker*, 14 December 1987.

190 Mario Praz, *An Illustrated History of Interior Decoration from Pompeii to Art Nouveau*, translated by William Weaver (London: Thames and Hudson, 1964).

216 The story of 'Prezzemolina' or 'Petrosinella' (Petrosinella, from the Neapolitan *petrosino*, for parsley; *prezzemolo* in Italiano) is drawn from Giambattista Basile's collection of folk tales, *Il racconto dei racconti or Il Pentamerone* (*Lo cunto de li cunti*, as it was first published in Italy, in 1634). The story of Rapunzel in her tower is a variation on the tale.

Illustrations

Acknowledgements

My thanks go to Danny, for everything, really, including
for first telling me the story that gave rise, in its sinuous
way, to this book; for giving me the key and supporting me,
with your intelligence and sensitivity, as I discovered all the
things it unlocked. To A for all that you are and will become,
and for the countless things you have already taught me
without words, without even knowing it.

To my parents and sister Helen. To my friends, all of you,
through time, and in particular to Emily Hill, for the tree hay
and the company, and Sophie Hughes, for reading me even
when I told her not to bother because she had a baby nestled
on her chest every hour of the day and night (because her
little I, like my A, was not really a sleeper).

To Katy de La Rivière (the admiral in blue) and Richard
Cann, at Sedbergh History Society, for their time and
generosity. To the elusive Brian for his off-the-cuff family
tree. To 'Mossy', 'Pompy', Carol, Jane and everyone else who
spoke to me up there. To Josh from Bereavement Services
for telling me to dig – it's good advice in general.

To Maxi Leigh and Kimberley Wilson for their knowledge of the brain and the mind and their weird workings. To
Stuart Sharp, at Lancaster University, for sharing his love of
dippers, and Judith Flanders for the insight into what 'good'
girls did in Annie's time.

To Jacques and the wonderful people at Fitzcarraldo
for letting me stumble around in the dark and being there for
whatever book I found.

Fitzcarraldo Editions
133 Rye Lane
London, SE15 4ST
Great Britain

Copyright © Thea Lenarduzzi, 2025
Originally published in Great Britain
by Fitzcarraldo Editions in 2025

The right of Thea Lenarduzzi to be identified as the
author of this work has been asserted in accordance with
Section 77 of the Copyright, Designs and Patents Act 1988.

ISBN 978-1-80427-179-7

Design by Ray O'Meara
Typeset in Fitzcarraldo
Printed and bound by Pureprint

All rights reserved. No part of this publication may be
reproduced, stored in a retrieval system or transmitted
in any form or by any means, electronic, mechanical,
photocopying, recording or otherwise, without prior
permission in writing from Fitzcarraldo Editions.

fitzcarraldoeditions.com

Fitzcarraldo Editions

The authorised representative in the EEA is eucomply OÜ,
Pärnu mnt 139b-14, 11317 Tallinn, Estonia.
hello@eucompliancepartner.com
+33757690241

This book is printed with plant-based inks on materials
certified by the Forest Stewardship Council®. The FSC®
promotes an ecologically, socially and economically
responsible management of the world's forests. This book
has been printed without the use of plastic-based coatings.